"Do not pigeonhole this book in the categories of lesbian or incest or recovery. Put it in the hands of every person who walks into your bookstore because that's who will enjoy—yes, I said enjoy—*SEARCHING FOR SPRING.*"

Mary Morell
Feminist Bookstore News

SEARCHING FOR SPRING

PATRICIA A. MURPHY

SEARCHING FOR SPRING

PATRICIA A. MURPHY

The Naiad Press, Inc.
1987

Printed in the United States of America
First Edition

Edited by Katherine V. Forrest
Cover design by The Women's Graphic Center
Typesetting by Sandi Stancil

Library of Congress Cataloging in Publication Data
Murphy, Patricia A., 1940—
    Searching for Spring.

    I. Title.
PS3563.U7484S4   1987   813′.54   87-11317
ISBN 0-941483-00-2

For my sisters and my daughter

Photo by Jamie Shoemaker and Lisa Rodriguez

ABOUT THE AUTHOR

Patricia A. Murphy has had many careers—vocational rehabilitation counselor, transcendental meditation teacher, women's studies instructor, nurse's aide, clerical worker, improvisational theater actor and artist's model.

She lives in Southern California with her poodle, her computer and a drawer filled with topographical wilderness maps. She has hiked or cross-country skied the California back country from Big Sur to the High Sierra.

Searching for Spring

Patricia A. Murphy

1

I am always searching for Spring. Perhaps it's because I am a child of the north country raised in a little house with too many people. Locked inside against the north wind which freezes the air in your lungs and attacks all your tips: the tip of your nose, the tip of the fingers and toes. The back of the neck. The top of the ears. Frosting the eyebrows. Even the eyes in the sockets are chilled. Searching for spring like the owls who return in February ignoring the temperature and following the light. The dark days of winter pass and the light returns little by little as the planet turns and we move toward the vernal equinox.

I am nine and I escape in the mornings before anyone else is up. I am out of the house with its dry coal-heated air and the odor of my father's cigarettes and whiskey. If I do not steal this time, then I will have none because after school I am expected to come home to help. In the summer, I am gone by five and back by seven. In the winter, I wait impatiently for the light, for the pre-dawn grey and gloom of the prairie sky and then I am off to the woods with its naked and twisted branches and twigs reaching upward for mercy.

I tramp through the snowdrifts to the quarry where the granite slabs are piled in crazy stacks all softened into hills of snow. The pond fed by underground water is still frozen and I stamp on its smooth snow-blanketed surface with confidence. I hurry across to the granite under a sheet of ice which encases the wall like a pane of clear glass. I peer closely into this bright ice searching for spring but I do not see any melting beneath. Disappointed, I turn in time to see a sleepy owl fly silently away; her great wings lazily flap. I will come back tomorrow and the next day and the next.

I am fascinated by thaw, by the water in the earth which slips even through granite and seeps silently down the face of the split stone under ice to the pond. And that warm melt dissolves the ice below and secretly spring creeps into the pond and then I will not be able to pound my feet anymore. I will have to tiptoe carefully around the edges to get to the wall and soon the sun will sparkle on the ice, the trickling water, the mica chips, and they will become a curtain of light dancing and dazzling my eye and I will believe in spring again.

But when I return to the house, I still have to deal with winter.

Have you ever seen small children outside in the winter? We five sisters and two brothers are surrounded by a vast silence into which falls the coldest and deepest of snow. All sensation is muffled. All sound, all touch, all scent. Our eyes are blinded with scarves and hoods and mufflers which push past our noses. Our fingers are stuck together under clammy woolen mittens. Our thumbs freeze in solitary horror. Our

2

toes are stuffed savagely into woolen stockings and shoes and boots over those; our balance is peculiar because we are unable to feel the ground with the bottoms of our feet. Some of us have just learned how to walk. We are unable to turn our heads because we are wearing an undershirt covered by a blouse and a sweater, a vest, and then a coat. Maybe somebody else's coat which is too small or has a rip down the back which we try to hide by walking sideways. Under the collar of the coat is a scarf and over that is a hat and sometimes there are earmuffs and so not only can't we turn our heads to see if there are monsters behind us, we are unable to raise our arms above our shoulders. Our knees are separated from each other by the wadding of our snow suits, our long underwear, our trousers and the woolen stockings which itch and crawl up over our knees.

We try to have fun by falling backward into a snow drift and waving our arms to make angel's wings. We need help to get back up and we secretly worry about falling forever into the soft cold snow, never to be seen again. Sometimes, one of the sisters loses a mitten, just because she wanted to feel something, and so the next time she goes out the mittens are attached by a string which runs through the arms of her coat across the back. It chafes at the windburned, chapped skin of the neck. We are all humiliated by this badge of babyhood.

When we stumble back into the house, we are greeted by Mother who is furious with us for being so much trouble. We melt puddles onto the clean, waxed kitchen linoleum. We cannot get out of all of our wrappings soon enough to suit her. We try desperately before she starts yelling and knuckle-rapping with her hand or her hair brush. The little ones start crying because now they are too hot and their cheeks are burning bright with windburn and their fingers are too young to untie scarfs or unfasten boots. Stella pees in her pants and wets through to her snowsuit.

3

The older ones help the younger ones. I quickly strip Stella before Mother finds out and I rinse the snowsuit in the bathroom sink and hang it on its peg in the porch hoping it will dry before Stella goes out again. Maggie helps DeeDee and now there are little piles of winter wrappings everywhere. Kathleen stands quietly in front of Mother who gently unwraps her like an unexpected gift. Bri helps no one and throws his jacket and boots into the porch behind the storm door and runs through the house shouting, "Yippee-yi-ya! Ride 'em cowboy!" Kevin has fallen into a corner on a pile of overcoats and jackets and he sniffles softly, his nose running with clear fluid.

And so even though I had been escaping them all as the years passed by (once I did not see any of them for five years—I was hiding in Southern California), when I called the meeting of my sisters, they came. They came because I was the oldest and what else could they do?

And wouldn't it be loverly if I could say that my four sisters and I came together on a houseboat on Trinity Lakes in Northern California and we had a marathon CR group which lasted three days and two nights and at the end of it we knew who we were, what everything meant and what to do about it? Like a CR group on rape or wife-battering where the famous feminist clicks and revelations leap out of somebody's mouth and suddenly everyone gets it. Or like group therapy where the leader hopefully knows what's going on.

It was Stella who suggested our meeting place. "Let's go to Trinity Lakes in Northern California," she told Kathleen. "It's a good compromise. Maggie can drive down from Seattle and you and I can drive from here north and maybe Annie will want to come with us. DeeDee is stuck no matter what we do." DeeDee was the only sister still living in the old hometown back in Wisconsin.

I flew to Las Vegas and Stella picked me up in one of her new cars, a 1980 Chrysler LeBaron. We drove to Mother's

4

apartment in Boulder City. Stella, Kathleen, and Mother had ended up in Boulder City, that improbable suburb facing Hoover Dam and the Colorado River, turning its back on its garish neighbor. DeeDee and Kathleen were waiting. They were all drinking Mother's inevitable Lipton tea with sugar and milk.

DeeDee and I hugged, which was harder than it sounds because she was seven months pregnant, with a belly the size of an over-inflated beach ball. She walked splayed like an overweight gorilla. She said that she had boils in her armpits which could not be lanced because of the fetus. She said her ankles swelled every night and she had heartburn but other than that she was fine. She said she hadn't even wanted this baby but one little sperm had apparently escaped the vasectomy. She said that abortion was out of the question and I wondered where she would get one anyway. The County of Storm Lake did not so much as sell rubbers in the drugstores. It was the Bishop's influence. "I think it's a girl," she said wistfully. "It's got to be. I have a boy and I want a girl. I deserve a girl and so it's a girl."

I immediately got out of my kitchen chair and knelt beside her. I pressed my left ear to her belly. "Hello little girl. I know you're in there or we wouldn't let you come on this trip."

Mother scolded, "Annie get up! How ridiculous. Really." Kathleen laughed nervously and Stella stared. DeeDee patted the top of my head.

I rose up and faced my Mother.

"Isn't it time to get on the road?" she asked me. "I'd sure like to be a mouse in the wall listening." But we did not invite her to come with us.

"I have to go to the bathroom one more time," DeeDee announced, clambering heavily out of her chair.

Stella and I drove together and the other two were behind us in Kathleen's station wagon. I said, "I think Mother's handling this pretty well, don't you?"

Stella glanced at me puzzled, "Handling what?"

"Not coming with us on this trip. All that."

She lit a cigarette and rolled down the window. "I suppose."

"It is a transfer of power after all from her to us." I contemplated my littlest sister. She wasn't my baby anymore. She was a whore. Not a conventional whore although her whoredom would prove to have classical foundations. She wasn't a call girl. Nor had she been on the streets. But she had kept her bartending job by fucking every important man in the posh hotel/casino where she held court as the undisputed queen of the Green Lounge in Las Vegas.

She had a baby of her own. A two-year-old boy, Jersey. This would be the first time she had left him overnight since his birth. Despite her parenting and the house in the suburbs surrounded by the desert, I thought we were bonded by our unmarried state, by our inability to conform. What I didn't understand was that, like all whores, Stella idealized marriage and aspired to it. She was envious of our three middle sisters and their traditional lives. She had even married once saying she might as well so that she could get divorced. Her child was not a product of her marriage but of an illicit love affair with a married man who had died in the crash of a small plane over the Colorado River. And now Stella and I were widow and divorcee, without the status of either.

I hadn't known I was acting out my dream of the rose-covered cottage and marriage until Laura left me and then I realized that I was enduring a divorce.

Our other bond was drugs, and so of course Stella and I were both high when we got to Trinity Lakes because we had been snorting cocaine on the way. I had a few joints stashed in my luggage and Stella and I agreed that we would try to get the others high. We also agreed that we wanted more respect from them. I proclaimed fervently, "Just because they're married doesn't make them better than us, more mature or

6

real or something." Neither of us paid any attention to the obvious contradictions in our self-created situation. With this righteous attitude, we rolled into the parking lot near the boat launch.

The first sister we saw was Maggie who walked toward us with the exaggerated gait of a sailor. The hat perched on her red curls labeled her CAPTAIN OF THE SHIP. "Captain," I muttered to Stella, "exactly what I was talking about." When Maggie handed us each a typed sheet of paper headed Rules of the Ship, Stella began to bristle.

I tried to read the rules with one eye and keep the other on Maggie. I heard Stella chortling and so I gave up and read, "Using your sister as an anchor is forbidden." I wondered what else was new. The second rule, "Walking on water is strongly encouraged." I understood that I had no sense of humor.

I glanced suspiciously at Maggie. As usual, she was about fifty pounds overweight but I knew she could take me out in a minute with her strong arms and her fierce energy. She was a woman of her times. What we called the re-entry woman in the late 1970s. It had taken her fifteen years to complete her bachelor degree in psychology and now she was ready: "Here's my B.A. . . where's the world?" She was giving her husband and two children the tasks of feeding themselves without pre-planned, pre-frozen meals for every day of the week. She even had the kids doing their own laundry.

When we were little, Bri used to push her into a corner and hold her there with one hand against her forehead. Her arms weren't long enough to reach him and he would laugh at her flailing fury. Her freckles would grow dark against her white skin, her blue eyes would fill with tears and her small fists were white-knuckled: She would scream and cry until he tired of the whole business and released her.

Now she was fighting death itself. She was Patient Services Coordinator for a hospice organization. She ran support groups for the dying and their families.

I stared at her, torn between admiration and suspicion, when DeeDee and Kathleen interrupted with shouts of, "Hello! Where's our boat? Did you have a good drive?"

"Great timing!" Maggie yelled back and the conversational level went up by a thousand decibels. It was always this way in the beginning. We were like five sirens going off and shutting down at separate intervals. If we were all rising at once, the noise was piercing. Some of it could be construed as conversation since there were actual words uttered and sentences constructed of shrieks, giggles, screams, belly laughs, moans, screeches and sudden, flat gaps of dead silence. These were always followed by some command to action such as "Let's get our room now," or "Park your car over there."

I decided that it was some sort of a riot as I found myself organized right into the best chair in our two-room suite in the motel as the guest of honor.

I searched Kathleen's elegant face for the child she had once been. She was a bottle-blonde now and it was not that ash-blonde shade I remembered so well from the 4th of July Parade when she was three and I was ten. We had all worn bathing suits with sashes and Maggie and I pulled Kathleen in a red wagon. As queen of the parade, a silver paper crown was placed on her cloud of baby hair. There is an old photograph of her squinting into the sun. She appears to be puzzled over the fuss and the crown has slipped, threatening to cover her left eye; she holds tightly to the sides of the wagon with both baby hands.

"Happy fortieth birthday," she said, putting a tiny silver-wrapped package into my hand as I sat in the overstuffed chair with my joke gifts of false teeth and shower cap. I tore away the glittering paper unsteadily and found a

8

velvet covered jewelry box. Inside a thin gold chain gleamed against white satin.

"It's beautiful," I whispered, wondering how they knew that my neck needed adorning. That my head had been pulled into my shoulders for months. That I had been sleeping in a hunched, cramped ball since Laura left. That my masseuse had pointed out that it was possible to put my shoulders down and my head up and that I had been practicing without much success.

Maggie plucked it out of the box and put it around my neck as I bowed my head. "It wasn't cheap," she said proudly.

The next morning we abandoned our motel room and moved into our houseboat. For the next three days and two nights we lived together on the sparkling, calm water.

Stella turned out to be the real captain of the ship. She hitched herself up onto the captain's stool in front of the wheel. Her feet did not touch the ground; she is only five-feet-one inch tall and the smallest of all of the sisters. Her face was scrunched up in concentration and pleasure as she chugged us into bays and inlets putting along at five miles per hour. I wanted to stick a cigar in her mouth.

Maggie and Kathleen unpacked groceries and laid out the first of days and days of feasts: a stuffed turkey was already baking in the oven. There were five cheeses—cheddar, gouda, Monterey Jack, French brie, strawberry cream cheese; fruits in season—grapes, plums, oranges, blueberries, honeydew melons, bananas, and a twenty-pound watermelon spiked with vodka; breads, cakes, crackers, and pumpkin muffins; salads—fruit with whipped cream and crisp romaine lettuce with mushrooms and cherry tomatoes. There was beer, diet coke, lemonade, gin, white wine, hot chocolate, and kahlua. There was coffee, cream, and cigarettes.

The cigarettes could only be smoked out of doors. Stella eyed the spiked watermelon morosely and informed us that she wasn't drinking anymore. I brought up getting high and

9

Stella moved closer to me, watching, and the three married sisters—Maggie, DeeDee and Kathleen—politely refused. DeeDee pointed out that she was pregnant and couldn't if she wanted to which she didn't. She pulled out a cigarette after this speech and went to the upper deck. Maggie and Kathleen seemed to wear the same disapproving frown. Maggie went to join DeeDee for a smoke and Stella and I stuffed our drugs back into our luggage and dropped the entire subject for the rest of the trip. Kathleen did not smoke, of course. She tidied up the galley instead.

We threw ourselves into the cool waters of the Trinity Lakes. We had our own bay and private beach and so we swam nude. We took pictures of DeeDee wearing nothing but an orange life jacket over her shoulders. Her swollen breasts and belly protruded pale white but she lowered herself into the water anyway and she and I had a fit of giggling out there in the lake. She tried to drown me by diving underneath me and pulling me down by grabbing my foot. She couldn't stay down very long because the life jacket bobbed her back up to the surface.

Later we all went to the top of the houseboat to sun ourselves. We compared bodies. We compared tits and asses and waists and weights and surreptitiously checked out each other's twats. I was keenly aware of being the oldest and of having to set the pace in the body beautiful sweepstakes. In the tit contest, I was second. Stella was first. Maggie, third. Maggie also had the pinkest of nipples and a glorious red bush which she carried about in her panties with smug knowingness. DeeDee and Kathleen were fourth and described their breasts as from the fried egg school. Kathleen complained about the length of her chest. She meant the distance from her throat to where her breasts started. DeeDee pointed out that her breasts were great now that she was pregnant but they would disappear again after the baby was born.

10

The turkey was reduced to bone and sandwich meat. Dishes had been washed and put away. We were down to coffee and pie. Maggie inhaled deeply and asked, "Why did you call this meeting anyway?"

"I didn't call this meeting," I protested. In fact, I had forgotten. My call had gone out and they had seized upon it with such fervor that I was able to pretend I hadn't called it. Husbands were firmly but gently reminded of all those hunting trips and business trips taken in the company of other adults. In those days, the mildest of housewives could explode into a rabid feminist tirade at the slightest slip of the lip.

"Yes, you did," DeeDee confirmed. The others nodded.

"Ummm," I grunted. I was afraid of them. In the motel they had given me a scrapbook filled with photographs of me and my life. I had managed the joke gifts and the gold chain, but the scrapbook had almost undone me.

I thought I had made the Great Escape and now here I was being dragged backward into time. I was used to not knowing anyone too well or for too long. In this way I would be safe, or so I thought. "I resign," I mumbled.

"What?" said Kathleen.

"What do you mean?" asked Stella, blowing cigarette smoke through the open window into the night air.

"I don't want to be the oldest anymore. I'm tired of being the oldest. I've been waiting and waiting for all of you to grow up and you have and so I resign."

Kathleen furrowed her smooth brow. Maggie leaned forward peering into my face. DeeDee shifted uncomfortably in her straight-backed chair. Stella lit another cigarette with her carefully painted nails, and that intensity peculiar to her rushed into her face and to her fingers and how she held the cigarette and brought it to her mouth. Her lips and nails thrummed with a tension so high pitched in frequency that it was beyond normal sight or hearing but it was there at the edges. We all leaned into it like people trying to hear a dog whistle.

"I'm lonely," I heard myself saying. "I need to change my life. Between Laura and the rape crisis center work and the battered women work." I shook my head. My throat was filled with tears, I could not speak. I gulped, "I mean, I think of it as love and terror. Laura jumped over my walls and got close to me and then we were exposed to so much violence, and then she left me."

"I told you it was too much," DeeDee stated flatly. "Remember when I told you?"

"You should talk!" I retorted, stung by her rebuke. "You've been involved in this stuff too. Putting together a battered women's shelter and a rape hotline."

"True enough," she acknowledged. "What do you mean, resign?"

"Yeah," said Maggie still studying me curiously.

"Dad used to put his hands on my breasts after dinner when we watched TV. Do you remember?"

Maggie's blue eyes widened. "No."

"Kathleen?"

"No."

"That's nothing," Stella announced. "Bri did more than that to me. Lots more." Her face fell into two pieces like masks not fitted properly to make a whole. There was one mask for the top of her face: the eyes and the nose, and another for the bottom: her mouth and chin. These two masks were incomplete and at war with each other and beneath the crack where the masks did not join was a glimpse into the being that was Stella. It was an abyss. "He paid me." She challenged DeeDee, "Didn't you ever wonder why I always had candy and money?"

DeeDee shifted in her chair so that her shoulder and part of her back rejected Stella. She turned her head to look back over her shoulder. "This is all in the past. So why bring it up?"

"Why are you so uptight all of a sudden, DeeDee?" I demanded, reverting to my role as the oldest.

"Well shit! Fuck and damn! I didn't want to come to this place anyway and now. . . ." She was out of her chair pacing the small cabin of the houseboat. She even stormed down the narrow passageway to the bunkroom. Returning, she blurted, "I have a secret I never thought I would share but I guess I have to now."

We waited. "It's Kevin. He came to me and told me all about it. He's molested Audrey." She was very pale. She took a cigarette from Stella's pack and lit up. All the rules about one person smoking at a time and then only out the window were forgotten. "Apparently he's been going to her room almost every night. He exposes his penis to her. He bought her a lock for her bedroom door and told her to lock herself in."

"How old is Audrey now?" Maggie inquired.

"Sixteen," DeeDee replied drily, pulling the smoke into her lungs.

"Kevin!" Stella snorted, lighting another cigarette even though another lay smoking in an ashtray propped near a window. "Him too. He did it to me too. And Bri hasn't stopped you know. I think he's been doing it to Carrie."

"My head hurts," Magggie said plaintively.

"Is it still going on?" Kathleen asked logically. "I mean if it's all in the past, why bring it up now?"

Stella and DeeDee started talking at the same time. They stopped and DeeDee glared at Stella who moved back into the shadows away from the light over the table. DeeDee continued, "Kevin took his family to counseling. He and Josie and the kids, Audrey and Melody."

"Not the little boy, K. Jr.?" Maggie asked.

"No, they thought he was too young. They've stopped going now, I guess. They didn't like the counselor." She paused, examining our astounded faces. "Well, they did try to get help." She was defensive now and tearful. "I promised not to tell."

"And Carrie too," Maggie said. "Is that still going on, Stella?"

"I don't know." She moved into the light.

"Is Carrie the same age as Audrey?" Kathleen folded a paper napkin into tiny squares.

"I think so," responded Maggie who kept track of things like that. "Our brothers have molested their own daughters. Is that what we're saying?"

I watched Stella mash cigarette butts into the amber glass of the ashtray. I felt very small and very big at the same time. I wanted to stay and be invisible but I felt exposed and yet not there. My little story seemed so unimportant. I pulled a yellow legal tablet out of my luggage under the bunkbed in the sleeping area. "Let's see if I understand this." I defaced several pieces of green lined paper before I got it right. "How do family trees work anyway?" They were muttering and mumbling all around me. Glasses were freshened. Ice pulled out of trays. Ashes dumped. The table was wiped around me as I worked. "Is this it?" I asked. All five of us crowded over my drawing.

Kathleen's porcelain skin was ivory white and taut like bone. "My god, Annie, that's not a family tree. It's a—"

"An incest tree," Maggie finished. "It's hard to be around you sometimes, Annie. The things you see." Nevertheless she hunched over my crude drawing with avid interest.

"How come you and I were never touched?" Maggie asked Kathleen. "Or were you?"

"Not me. Not DeeDee either, right?" Kathleen glanced up at DeeDee standing behind her.

"Right." DeeDee affirmed, lips tightly pressed together.

"How long have you known about Kevin and his daughter?" I asked her.

14

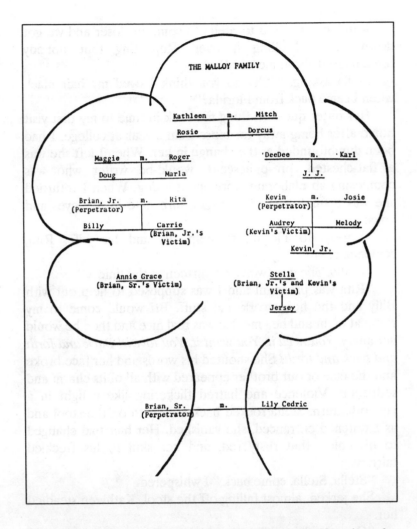

THE MALLOY FAMILY

Kathleen — m. — Mitch
Rosie — Dorcus

Maggie — m. — Roger
Doug — Marla

DeeDee — m. — Karl
J. J.

Brian, Jr. — m. — Rita
(Perpetrator)
Billy — Carrie
(Brian, Jr.'s Victim)

Kevin — m. — Josie
(Perpetrator)
Audrey — Melody
(Kevin's Victim)
Kevin, Jr.

Annie Grace
(Brian, Sr.'s Victim)

Stella
(Brian, Jr.'s and Kevin's Victim)
Jersey

Brian, Sr. — m. — Lily Cedric
(Perpetrator)

"Two, three years," she replied settling herself back at the table again.

"My God, DeeDee!" Maggie exclaimed. "I'm so sorry you've had to carry that all by yourself." Maggie pulled out a chair and sat down beside her, brushing the hair back from DeeDee's cheeks. DeeDee turned her face away.

15

Kathleen gestured to Stella to come in closer and we got down to it. Mulling it over. Repeating that nobody remembered about me and Dad.

Stella asking, "Why do you think I dyed my hair black when I came back from Florida?"

Her bitter question flung me back in time to my first visit home after being away for more than a year at college. I had been dumbfounded at the change in her. When I left she was a flat-chested, pre-pubescent, would-be writer who was composing an elaborate story about a dog. When I returned she was a full-bosomed teenager with hate in her eyes and voice.

"I went to Florida to help Bri and his wife, Rita, remember?"

We did. She was twelve or thirteen at the time.

"Rita was pregnant and I was supposed to help out with Billy and the housework and stuff. Bri would come to my room at night and beg me. He was real nice and then he would get angry. *You need it. You want it. You love it! Back and forth and back and forth!* She shouted his words and her face broke and the face of our brother appeared with all of its charm and seduction. Violence and hatred flickering like a light in a jack-o-lantern. Stella rocked back and forth on the stool and as I watched entranced, she vanished. Her hair had changed to his color, that rusty red, and her skin to his freckled fairness.

"Stella, Stella, come back," I whispered.

She jerked, almost falling off the stool. Kathleen steadied her.

"Once he demanded sex with both Rita and me together. And now he's doing it to Carrrie. What a fool I am."

Kathleen reached out to touch her but Stella shrugged away indignantly.

16

DeeDee stood up so abruptly her chair fell over with a clatter. She picked it up awkwardly and righted it. "I'm going to bed. I'm exhausted and I can't take any more."

We cleaned up the galley and prepared ourselves for sleep. We were anchored in a tiny inlet and the soft waves of the lake beat gently against the pebbled shore. The stars gleamed through the light mist in the night sky as we brushed our teeth and washed our faces in an unsteady silence broken only by the night calls of birds and the song of crickets. The houseboat swayed in the calm water as we climbed into our bunk beds in the darkness. All five of us in a space eight-by-five feet. Kathleen and Stella were pressed together in one bunk.

As I lay back in my lower bunk with Maggie above me, I asked the question which had been crushing us all, "What about Mother? Where was she when all of this was going on?"

The question went out into the dark air and hung there like a specter. Blackness gathered and grew and I felt flattened, suffocated, but no one answered.

I woke with the sun in my eyes and Maggie standing over me in her white cotton nightgown, her uncombed red hair spread out around her head like points on a crown. Her blue eyes were filled with fury. "I really resent this, Annie. Bringing Mother into all of this. You're just trying to take over, that's all." There was a muttered chorus of agreement behind her.

Exhaustion crept up on me. It was a familiar feeling. I even welcomed it like an old friend. There was nothing to say. I lay flat on my back in the bunk bed imprisoned by Maggie. I stared straight ahead at the wire springs of the bed above me. I waited. The chorus grew louder. "Yeah, who do you think you are?" I waited.

When Maggie realized that I wasn't going to speak, she continued, "Well, you're not the only one who knows stuff around here, you know. I have leadership skills too and I'm not going to let you take over here. I won't."

I pushed my chin down to my chest because I didn't want her to see my smile or hear the chuckle deep in my chest. I wondered if she was going to stamp her foot. "Okay, Maggie," I managed to get out.

"Okay?" she repeated in a bewildered tone. She looked around for help but they had abandoned her for the kitchen. Coffee was brewing. She grumbled her way into the tiny bathroom and freed me from my prison.

All through breakfast Maggie eyed me dubiously but I steadfastly refused to be baited. DeeDee, Kathleen and Stella avoided all but the most basic of interaction. Maggie took a deep breath and said, "Let's go up onto the roof."

We followed her obediently up the short ladder, helping DeeDee from the top and from behind as she hoisted her heavy body topside.

It was a glorious summer morning. The sun hot and fresh on the deck and the cool lake water gleaming like a blue polished stone. The green needled pines stood guard over the shoreline beyond.

Maggie had come prepared. She handed out paper and pencils and asked us to trace our hands on the paper. "I want us to do something positive." She glared at me in challenge but I meekly tried to take the note pad from her grip.

"You have to let go of it, Maggie," I said gently.

"Oh!" She let go.

As we laid our hands on the paper, I wondered what it was with Maggie and hands. A few weeks before the trip she had mailed me a legal-sized piece of paper. When I unfolded it, I realized that it was a photo copy of three palm prints; each distinct from the other. I did not need names written underneath each print. There was Maggie's daughter's palm, so narrow and young with its delicate fingers and fresh lines cutting around the edges. Maggie's hand, fleshy and rounded with the lines inside muted and crisscrossed with experience, life. And Mother's palm. It was old. The life line and the heart

18

line were all interconnected by a thousand tiny and unsuspected cracks and fissures suddenly uncovered by a copying machine.

As I shook myself away from my contemplation and completed my assignment, Maggie directed us to pass the hands to each other. "I want you to write something you admire about each sister in one of the fingers or the thumb. Stella, put your name on your hand." Kathleen took her own drawing back from me and wrote her name on it. When we had ourselves sorted out, Maggie added, "When you get your hand back, write something you like about yourself, in whatever is left, a thumb or finger."

When my hand came back there were comments in the fingers such as, "brave and smart."

I don't know what I did with the drawing. I've lost it and I can't find it anywhere, in any of my papers or journals. I can't remember what I wrote in anybody's fingers but I do remember us taking our hands back with a kind of hopelessness, a clutching of the papers to our collective and individual bosoms with the hand side of the paper toward our hearts as a private matter too important to casually leave lying about face up somewhere and too tender to expose. Even to those who had expressed their love.

I wrote, "I love myself" in the space my thumb print created. I didn't, but it was a start anyway.

"Well, this is all very nice but what are we going to do?" Stella asked this bitterly, leaning back on her elbow as she stretched out bare-breasted on the deck, dragging cigarette smoke into her lungs. She addressed her question to Maggie. Kathleen and DeeDee glanced at each other and then at me but I averted my eyes.

"What we are going to do today is have a nice time and not worry about any of this," she pronounced. She pulled her hat firmly down around her brow and I noticed that freckles were popping out on her bare shoulders. She spread suntan lotion on her pale breasts.

"Well, I'm going for a swim." With that I stripped off my caftan and jumped into the lake off the roof of the houseboat making a huge splash as I pulled my knees up to my chest in a cannonball plunge. I came up screaming because I had fallen into one of the cold pockets in the eddies and streams of the lake. They laughed and I dove down in a shallow arc, breast-stroking to warmer water. When I came up I saw DeeDee lowering herself into the water from a ladder over the side. Her buttocks were pale moons flushed with a light sunburn. The orange lifejacket rode high on her shoulders. I side-stroked over to her. "Hello! Naked pregnant woman," I shouted.

"Ha! You should talk. You're wearing a gold chain around your neck and nothing else. Do you think you will ever take it off?"

"Probably not," I replied, treading water. We faced each other. She had less work to do because of the lifejacket.

"Are your breasts smaller than they used to be?" She was wearing her Huck Finn grin.

I splashed her. "What a weird question! Why do you ask?" She splashed back and got me in the face. I sank beneath the water and rose up eyes closed, nose pointing skyward, hair slicked back.

"I heard Maggie and Kathleen talking. They think your boobs are smaller than they used to be."

I treaded water, pumping with my legs. I moved water back and forth with my hands. I sank down so that only my head was revealed. "I wear a thirty-four C bra size which is what I have worn since I was fifteen or sixteen years old. I think what it is is because of Dad fondling my breasts in front of everybody while we watched TV after supper—everybody got obsessed with my breasts. After all, I was the first one to grow them." I sank deeper, to my lower lip. "You know how

20

people say everything looks smaller when they come back and look at it as adults? Most people are talking about a house where they lived. In my case, it's my breasts." And with that I sank all the way down into the water and dived into the murky depth of the lake. Darker and darker. Colder and colder.

When I surfaced she said, "We'll have to do something, won't we?"

"I'm afraid so."

We paddled around unenthusiastically for a while and I tried to float on my back which never works because my feet sink. When we rejoined the others in the galley for soup and hot tea, it was clear that a conference was in session. Stella announced that she would invite Bri's daughter, Carrie, for a visit. "And then I'll ask her if he is doing to her what he did to me." She tapped her long gleaming nails on the table top. She pulled her white terry cloth robe tight around her torso.

Maggie put her hand on DeeDee's shoulder. "I'm coming back to Storm Lake next month for Roger's parents' wedding anniversary. Why don't you and I go together and confront Kevin? We need to find out if it's still going on with Audrey."

DeeDee shook Maggie's hand away. She wrapped the towel around her wet hair like a turban. "I promised I wouldn't tell," she said fearfully, jaw trembling.

"I'll be with you," Maggie repeated.

"Annie, if Carrie says yes, then I want you to take on Bri. You can handle him." Stella's voice was harsh with smoke and tension.

There was no assignment for Kathleen and she did not ask for one. We settled into an afternoon of cards: poker, whist, canasta, pinochle and hearts. When the long shadows cast by the mountain peaks lay across the still, gentle waters of the lake, we pulled mattresses and blankets up the ladder to the upper deck. Nobody spoke of the night mist which seemed to gather in the bunkroom and hang there sucking air.

It was our last day. Kathleen methodically folded bathing suits and towels. She baked muffins in the miniature oven and scrambled eggs. She served us breakfast on paper plates with carefully sliced avocado slices artistically placed between the steaming muffins and the fresh yellow of the eggs. We complimented her on her cuisine and we tacitly understood that Kathleen was our diplomat. Her assignment was to handle Mother when the fallout began.

2

Stella called me at home three weeks after the houseboat trip. She was sputtering with fury. "It's true. It's all true! It's even worse than I thought."

"Why?" I asked.

"Because he had intercourse with her. It was more than he made me do."

"Oh."

"She wears a tampax all the time."

"Carrie does? Why does she do that? Oh."

"Yeah. She says she feels cold without it but the thing is—she has an infection and I can't get her to the doctor with me." Stella's voice was hoarse with smoking and frustration. "I keep nagging her."

"It's not so crazy, is it? Menstruation and infection. A good way to keep him off her, right?'

"Right."

I remembered toxic shock syndrome. "I suppose you'll have to get her there whether she likes it or not."

"Oh sure, I'll just throw her over my shoulder and drag her off. Oh God!"

"What?"

"I just remembered. She had an infection, a vaginal infection when she was ten or so. I was living with them at the time and I took her to the doctor. It was going on then. I'm such a fool."

I noticed that I was holding the telephone receiver so tightly my hand was aching. "What about now?"

"She says no but when they went to Europe last year he propositioned her and she refused."

We hung together on the phones in silence for a while. "Will she go for counseling?"

"Absolutely not." I heard the sucking intake of air and smoke and then she added, "It's your turn now. Call Bri and tell him we have Carrie and we are going to keep her."

I wanted Laura. I wanted Laura. I turned to find her and then I remembered she was gone. She was living in her yellow room with the high ceiling and the white curtains blowing over the long narrow windows. She was living in a room with a double bed in it and there were women in that bed but not me. I was living in the stucco cottage we had found together. I stared at the maps on the wall. Los Padres National Forest, Lake Tahoe, the London subway system. "What are you looking for?" she had asked me one day when she stopped by for a visit. She walked up to the map of the Pacific Ocean floor. "Do you find it here?"

"I just haven't found the right map yet," I had replied, knowing that in addition to the ones on the walls there were three drawers full in my lonely bedroom.

I picked up the phone. I dialed Bri's work number and he answered. I was so surprised I almost dropped the receiver. He was a tenured professor at a local state university, a political scientist. His government work kept him circling the globe. He was one of those people who really live nowhere because they are always on their way to somewhere else. "This is Annie," I announced.

"Hello," he answered and waited, offering nothing. I could envision him settling back in his upholstered office chair with his pipe and his little belly popping out on his slender frame. His hair was darker, almost auburn now, the beard a shade lighter than his hair.

"We have Carrie."

And he said, "What did she tell you?"

And I thought, we have always known this. He and I and Stella and everybody. In some way, we have always known. What I said was, "Nothing. She didn't have to tell us anything. We figured it out and asked her.

"How does she feel about me?" His question slammed me up against the wall of my own naivete. This was a question a lover asks, not a parent. "How does she feel about me?" He repeated impatiently.

"She loves you and she hates you. What do you think?" I just knew he was wearing one of those Brooks Brothers three-piece suits Carrie had picked out for him.

"You have no right. You're no professional."

"I have the right, Bri. Dad did it to me. I have the right."

That silenced him for a beat but then, "You're no professional," he repeated.

I broke. "Get help, Bri. Get help. I tell you this not to hurt but to heal." There were hot tears in my eyes.

"I've been getting help for this long before you ever came along." There was a sneer in his voice now.

"We're keeping Carrie," I said, but he hung up and when I tried to call him back I got a busy signal.

I took a tour of my maps on the wall of the living room. I decided for the one hundredth time that my favorite was the Lake Tahoe. Something about the shape of the lake. I paced the cottage returning to the phone, and after several calls I was directed to the Los Angeles County Department of Social Services.

A pleasant, well-educated man with a soft southern accent was assigned to my call. "These guys are usually grateful once it's out and they're over the initial anger," he informed me.

"But he told my sister Stella only yesterday he was going to cut my tits off. I'm afraid."

"Now listen to what I'm telling you. They are grateful. The burden of the secret is lifted. It's a relief."

"How long does it take between anger and gratitude?" I wanted to know. I spoke into the phone with my arms mashed against my chest. I couldn't spend my life checking to see if my breasts were still there.

He ignored my question and gave me instructions for calling the police. "It's very important that you turn him in."

"Why?"

"Because otherwise these guys don't think they did anything wrong. When they go to jail, they begin to realize how serious it is."

"Okay," I said doubtfully.

I called Bri again that night at his house. "I've talked to the professionals and they advise me to turn you in to the police. They've also told me to tell you this."

Icy silence.

I continued, "The other thing you should know is, Kevin has molested his daughter too. Audrey. She's the same age as your Carrie." I was babbling into his not speaking.

He cut in, "You shouldn't have told me that." His voice was so cold I shivered.

I called my social worker again the next morning. I filled him in and he praised me. "Good. Good. Now tell me more about your brother."

"Ah, well. He's a professor at Long Beach State University and he has a law degree from Stanford and—"

"He's an attorney?"

"I guess so but he doesn't practice that much. He's—"

"Where did the alleged molestations take place?"

"Alleged?"

"Where did it happen?"

"Different places, I guess. Europe, San Francisco, Los Angeles, Hawaii. I don't know. Does it matter?"

He mumbled something about jurisdictional problems and left the phone promising to get back to me the very next day. When he didn't call, I called him but he was out. Out on a case. Out to lunch. In conference. Out.

Since the professionals had abandoned me and I was left holding my tits, so to speak, I went to the semi-professionals. A meeting of Parents United. I walked right into a meeting of mothers and fathers and daughters. The fathers were men who had been in jail for perpetrating incest on their daughters and their participation in this self-help group was part of their probation. None of their own daughters were present, I noticed, but each man had his wife by his side.

One woman held her husband's hand and said, "I just thought they were close." A man pointed out, "Female infanticide is a common practice in many cultures and for good reason too." When I protested this, one of the wives remarked "This is not a feminist meeting."

Curiously enough I told my story and not Carrie's. Perhaps it was because Carrie's mother had abandoned her long ago. Nobody knew where Rita was but I had a mother and I knew exactly where she was. "Have you talked to your father about this? asked one of the men.

"Why would I do that? His brain is pickled in alcohol. I don't think there's anybody home."

His wife interjected, "Are you making this up?"

I went home. I took a long, long shower. When the hot water ran out, I put on levis and a t-shirt, and cleaned the kitchen. Then swept the sidewalk in front of the cottage and after that raked the leaves in the backyard in the dark. When enough time had passed for the hot water heater to do its work, I took another shower. Then washed my hair. Got my clothes ready for the laundromat. I tried to read and when the sun came up, I went to bed.

Maggie called the next morning. "I'm back home. DeeDee and I talked to Kevin. Josie was in on it too. We all sat in the living room which is so clean I would feel comfortable eating off the rug. Kevin has put on so much weight; he's got quite the beer belly now. Josie still has her blond hair. I think she does it for him. Bleach it, I mean."

"Well?" Enough of this social history. I wanted the news.

"You know how he is. He agreed it was all very serious and he would certainly need to go into counseling again. Then Audrey came in and—"

"Audrey was there?"

"Oh yes, and he asked her if she felt she needed any more counseling."

"And she said no," I finished cynically.

"Right. And Josie said she didn't need any either and everything was fine. Just fine and dandy."

A sudden vision of Josie and her daughter bobbing their heads at each other like little bright jerky birds chirruping, "Fine and dandy. Fine and dandy. Fine and dandy."

"Did you tell them about Bri and Carrie?"

"Yes, and we urged Kevin to reach out to Bri and he promised to think it over." She sighed.

"And DeeDee? Is she okay?"

"I think she's glad it's over."

"And you?"

"Annie, do you think this is really necessary? Bringing all this out into the open?"

"I don't know," I told her. I filled her in on my confrontation with Bri.

"I don't think he really meant that about your breasts, do you?"

"Oh Maggie, you want everything to be nice."

"Of course I do."

I didn't tell her about the Parents United Meeting. Stella's call came right after Maggie's and I was beginning to wonder if I would have a telephone permanently attached to my ear.

"I'm sending Carrie to you," she announced. "I can't handle her. All she cares about is money and clothes. I can't stand it. Pick her up at LAX at five p.m., okay?"

"I guess. You're sure?"

"She's driving me nuts. Take her."

"Okay, okay."

She slammed the phone down and I went into the room I had been preserving for Laura. Just in case she decided to come back. A room for her flute and guitar. A forlornly naked music stand waited for her. I collapsed its metal parts into a bundle of shafts and put it on the top shelf of the closet. I removed old clothing from the chest of drawers and made up the single bed with my best sheets. Opened the windows so that the air would be sweet and fresh with a tang of salt in it from the ocean.

Carrie was a delicious sixteen-year-old beauty with slanted oriental eyes and silky black hair, gifts from her Philippine mother. A sprinkling of freckles revealed her Celtic heritage as did her pug nose. She stoically set herself up in the bedroom I had prepared for her. She had two fears. "Am I pretty?" she asked. It turned out that she was worried about her nose.

I took her to the photographs of the family reunion where Laura stood next to me smiling forever. But it was Stella I pointed out to Carrie.

"See? Your nose is like hers and she's a beautiful woman."

The next day I noticed that she was making trips between the photograph and the bathroom mirror. When I heard a tiny satisfied sigh, I stopped worrying. I stopped worrying even though she wouldn't tell me anything about why she and Stella didn't get along.

Her other fear took longer to surface. She was standing in front of the photograph again when I came down the hall. "Were you and Laura married or whatever?" She did not look at me when she asked this, keeping her face to the wall.

I stood beside her looking at the photograph. "You could say that."

"Do you miss her?"

"Yes, I miss her all the time."

She faced me now. "Then you're a—you're gay? Right?"

"Right."

"Do you think I'm gay; because of what happened between Dad and me?" And although she was maintaining her teenage cool, I glimpsed her vulnerability. There was a softening around her eyes.

"Let's go sit down," I suggested. I lay on the floor and studied my map of Lake Tahoe. "Well," I said thoughtfully, "you don't feel like a baby dyke to me." I waited a beat or two and then I swung around just in time to see her break into giggles. "And besides, I don't think the two things have anything to do with each other."

"Really?" She was serious now.

"Really."

"I was worried."

"I know."

"In that case it would be okay if I were gay then, because it wouldn't be about that."

We smiled at each other. This was the first time she had ever referred directly to the incest.

"What do you want, Carrie? I don't have the money I need to take care of you the way I'd like to and your father says he can't send much. You're a young adult and I think you need to be part of the decisions here."

"He doesn't have much money," she confirmed, sitting with one hand cupping the other. "Maybe I should go back to Stella's."

And then it fell together neatly as a folded Japanese fan. Bri would send money to Stella but not to me. Stella was still his in the same way that Carrie was his but Stella and Carrie could not live together because Carrie had replaced Stella as the queen in my brothers's stable of whores. I raised my eyes to Carrie. She returned my scrutiny calmly, her dark head framed by the green of the map of the Ventana Wilderness.

I consulted my attorney friends and they gave me the bitter truth. I would be lucky to get two hundred dollars per month out of Bri if I won custody which was highly unlikely given my lifestyle. Carrie pointed out that if some decision wasn't made soon, she would hold me responsible for screwing up her entire junior year. She wanted to be class president.

Bri came that Friday and took her home with him. He and I stood in the driveway while she packed her things into the back seat of the car. It was a bright summer day with sunwashed blue skies, and I noticed that I wasn't feeling anything. Maybe that's why it was so easy to chat about the weather with him and say goodbye to Carrie as though she had just stopped by for a visit. We didn't mention my breasts.

That afternoon I ran into a candy-apple-red VW bug while crossing Main Street. I didn't run into it with my car. I walked into it as it moved slowly down the street. I bounced back onto the pavement ending up in prayer position before the passenger side, and the driver leaped out of the little bug in a panic crying, "Are you okay?"

Struggling to my feet, I waved him off. But someone had been at my knees with a hammer. "I'm fine. I'm fine. I'm fine and dandy," I repeated and repeated.

He drove away shaking his head and I staggered to a bus stop bench and sat down. "There's something wrong here, Malloy," I advised myself. My left kneecap throbbed. "You just tried to kill yourself without looking." The other kneecap joined in. "Do you want to kill yourself?" I trembled in the sunlight as I sat on the bright blue bench.

By nightfall my knees were black with bruises and I remembered Scarlet O'Hara in her dirt patch clutching dust and crying out, "I'll never be poor again!"

"Scarlet, my girl," I said, "you may have something there."

I made a list of the people who had been after me to write grants, procedural manuals and computer templates for word processing. As I lowered myself carefully into the steaming bath water, I screamed at the ceiling, "Screw my vow of poverty!"

I had taken this vow at the tender age of eighteen when I decided never to marry. I was unable or unwilling to make a modest little living as a secretary or teacher or nurse and so I lurched from college to odd jobs, ending up finally at the University where I thought I had found my ideal occupation: running a women's center.

I suppose I was on another search for spring. Working at the University was like slogging through the muck and mire of the March wood in order to find the first violets, yellow-centered, surrounded by furry green leaves.

But Laura was what I found at the University. On the first year anniversary of her leaving me the opal fell out of the ring she had given me. I replaced the stone with an amethyst. I used to refer to it as my purple heart but my perennial nine-year-old self knew that I was commemorating spring.

32

3

By the end of the next week, I settled into the business of making money. The weeks and months went into fast forward. I was successful at my computer consulting work beyond my most preposterous expectations.

I moved to a condominium in the mountains near Malibu State Park. I ran in the forest on the trails in the morning. I ran when the forest was wet with dew sparkling on all the leaves and grasses. I came back soaked with the fragrance of the wild. One morning as I skipped over rocks and through stream beds, stooping under low hanging branches, I knew myself as animal. One with the forest. There was no separation between my running, my breathing, and the buds and flowers and branches. The stream, the birds, the butterflies and me. We flowed and I could make no mistakes. Of course, the moment I became aware of this unity, I lost it and became human again.

My forty-second birthday approached. Almost two years had passed since the meeting on the houseboat. I found the making of money an absorbing distraction. I was looking forward to a lazy summer in the state park and an increasing bank account when Bri called me at my office. I was parked in front of my IBM PC, designing templates for a management consulting firm. When the call came through, I made a careful note on my billing ledger. My fee was one hundred dollars per hour and I didn't want to lose a penny.

"Hello," I said pleasantly. I was mildly curious.

"Carrie is graduating from high school this week and we would like you to come to the ceremony." A seductive charm poured through his silken baritone. When I didn't respond he added, "She won a scholarship to Mills College."

I was still speechless. What did he want? I gathered myself together. "When is it?"

"Sunday at noon. Meet us in the parking lot. You have to have a ticket to get into the stadium." He gave me the directions.

It was a bright June day in Newport Beach. The green grass of the football field was an emerald carpet below the bleachers where I sat with Carrie's brother, Billy. Bri was dressed in one of his six-hundred-dollar suits. Billy and I searched the rows of graduates in their royal blue caps and gowns for a glimpse of Carrie. Bri wandered off with his camera, instructing us to save him a seat. Billy and I peered through the binoculars searching unsuccessfully for Carrie in the milling crowd below.

"Annie!"

I looked up and Brenda stood there with an armload of red roses. Brenda was an ex-lover of Bri's and like Laura she was stuck in the family reunion photographs smiling forever. I had thought the relationship over long ago. She was married to someone else now and there was a baby, wasn't there? "What are you doing here?" I blurted rudely. What the hell was going on?

She sat down importantly. "The roses are for Carrie. Do you think she'll like them?"

"Of course!" I responded irritably. I was being used—but for what? "How's the baby?"

She brightened. "I have a picture. Just a minute." She put the roses down and pulled a set of photographs out of her purse. "She's eighteen months already and walking and talking. Isn't she beautiful?" And while I looked at baby cheeks, fat little hands, curly black hair and bright eyes, she whispered, "We're seeing each other again."

"You and Bri?" I said stupidly. Billy studiously ignored the two of us whispering over the photographs. He adjusted the binoculars. "What about your husband?"

"Andy's upset, of course." But she didn't sound upset at all. She sounded happy. "It's really, really good, Annie." She looked at me hopefully.

Before I could react to this astonishing piece of news, Bri was back and the ceremony was underway and the *Star Spangled Banner* was playing and we all stood up. I put my hand on my heart. We stood for the processional. I left my hand on my heart. Bri leaned over Brenda and said to me, "You and Brenda should really get together for lunch."

"Oh yes! Let's do!"

In the parking lot after the ceremony, I hugged Carrie and gave her a check for one hundred dollars. I escaped attending the graduation party by pleading a business appointment. "On Sunday?" they asked. "Yes," I replied, promising to meet with Brenda the following Wednesday.

We met at Bruno's Italian Restaurant in Culver City. The setting was appropriately dramatic. It was like having lunch in a cathedral. We tried to ignore it by downing two glasses of Chablis as quickly as possible. I did shift my chair slightly so that the floating angel in the twelve-foot painting to my left wasn't staring down into my antipasto. We chatted mindlessly through lunch and didn't get down to it until the cappuccino. I examined her, thinking that she was prettier than she used to be. She was wearing a lilac silk blouse with a dark blue skirt which showed off her narrow legs. She was soft, trim, and hysterical.

"I am so confused. I'm thinking of marrying Brian and I've asked Andy to leave the house."

I wondered why I was the recipient of this information except that Bri's women always confessed to me before they left him. I was never sure if they were responding to the lesbian within me or my aspect of Bri as female. The sun streamed through the cathedral windows and I wished for stained glass. I switched to wine.

"I'm seeing Brian's psychologist and so is Andy."

"You're all seeing the same therapist?"

"Brian wanted me to go." She ordered another bottle of Chablis from the hovering waiter.

"Is this the shrink he's been seeing for years?"

"Yes, I think so."

She looked at her watch. "I have to get back to the office. Aren't you going to say something to me?"

My ears were on fire. I wanted to look into a mirror and see if they were red. "What is it you want from me?" I asked. "I don't understand why I'm here." We had never been friends and we had not continued our relationship after she and Bri had separated. She wasn't as helpless as his usual women. She was more like me and Maggie than any of the others.

"There's something you're not saying, Annie. What is it?"

I didn't want to tell her.

"Just spit it out!" she commanded, stumbling over the "s" in "spit."

"How much do you know about Bri?" I ventured cautiously.

"Well, I lived with the man for three years. I think I know his oddities." She was smug and possessive.

"What oddities, Brenda?" I seized upon the word. I wanted her to inform me.

"I know he likes really young women." Her effort at composure collapsed into haggardness. "Just tell me."

I remembered that she had a small daughter. "Do you know about his relationship with Carrie?"

Her eyes flickered like the shutter of a camera catching the precise moment of the sun moving through the clouds. A small movement but really quite violent in its speed and accuracy. There was no surprise. I waited and we sat quietly. The restaurant emptied of the lunch crowd. The waiters drifted in the background. I was aware of white linen. She put her napkin on the table with careful concentration. "I have suspected. It's all making sense. The therapist's hints. She knows! She's always known. Why didn't she tell me?"

I wasn't kind. "How could she? She has to protect Bri."

She put her face into her hands and I told her everything I knew about all of us. "Come with me, Annie. I just can't go alone. I'm to see Ida at four today. Please!"

I saluted the angel to my left. It was St. Michael, the Archangel. He drove Satan out of paradise. "I wouldn't miss it for the world," I told her.

Ida lived high on a hill above the ocean, in a castle with stone walls and windows with iron bars. The driveway was as big as a parking lot. Brenda opened the door to a hallway with a curving staircase leading to the upper levels of the house. There were doorways everywhere. All the doors were shut. It was curiously institutional like a jail or a hospital. Brenda chose the door to the right. Ida was on the other side and she opened it abruptly to Brenda's knock. She was a short, plump woman with dark curly hair and a saturnine face. She looked like a bookish housewife. Her mouth quivered between some sort of fatal weakness and deep strength. The room was cluttered with papers, files, and books. It was difficult to move because of the two huge desks, three upholstered easy chairs and an oversized sofa. Plastic quart bottles of 7-Up littered the desk tops. "Who's this?" she challenged.

I was feeling tall. I was taller than Brenda and the psychologist. I was glad that she was short and dumpy.

"This is Brian's sister, Annie. I asked her to come with me today." I admired Brenda's calm reply.

Ida gestured us to seating and I stumbled around one of the heavy desks and ended up on the sofa across from Brenda who was swallowed by the easy chair. Ida sat between us, her features etched with disapproval. "Why didn't you let me know?"

Brenda hitched herself up onto the edge of the chair but before she could answer, the telephone rang and Ida answered it. Then her son came to the door and she took care of him. I leaned to Brenda. "She's buying time. Does she do this in all of your sessions?"

"Yes."

"Call her on it. You are paying for her time." I wanted Brenda to keep her spine straight.

Ida came back and sat down. There was an awkward silence. Brenda squared her thin shoulders. "Annie's told me everything about Brian and Carrie. What I want to know is why you didn't tell me?"

I knew that Ida was aware of my scrutiny. "I've been working on this all week," she said defensively. "I even called the American Psychological Association in Washington, D.C. and they are sending me a copy of the Incest Reporting Act passed by Congress. I couldn't tell you. I had to protect his confidentiality. Haven't you suspected? I've been dropping you hints as best I could."

Brenda hung her head. "Yes."

"Then you broke the rules, didn't you? The rule of not withholding anything. You tied my hands." She slapped her hands across each other and I thought, *Pontius Pilate!*

I spoke for the first time. "And what about you, Ida? Where's your responsibility to Carrie? Why didn't you protect her when she needed it? You knew this before anyone else."

The battle was joined. "What do you mean?"

"You know exactly what I mean."I spelled it out for her. "Bri has used you to justify his behavior by saying that he's been getting professional help. So what? The beat goes on. What about Brenda's daughter?" She flinched. "Bingo! Your career is endangered by this one, huh. Too many people know about Bri. It's not like it was before with Carrie all alone."

She ignored me and went after Brenda who was shaking. "I've had a little spat with Brian. I told him that he had to tell you. He wanted me to convince you to marry him."

I laughed. They both jumped, startled by this harsh sound. "It's perfect. Just perfect. He's used us all."

"And what about you?"

I saw the strength in her eyes. That piercing quality which all psychologists must have if they are to be any good. "What do you mean?" I tried to recall that I was five-foot-six and she was probably four-foot-eight.

"What do you want out of this?"

"I want him to get well. I want this to be over. I want the family to be well."

"No, no. You. What do you want?" Her emphasis was on the 'you' which she pushed at me like a sword.

But I could smell her fear. It stank worse than my own. "I have stated what I want as clearly as I can."

She shrieked, "You hate Brian! You want to destroy him! But he's a human being and," she finished feebly, "he has to pay for Carrie's therapy."

"Oh yeah, Carrie's therapy. What therapy? Why should she trust you or any shrink?"

"You want to destroy his career!"

"I don't hate Bri," I said sadly, wishing I did. It would be easier.

"What about me?" The little voice squeaked. We had both forgotten about Brenda.

"What about Carrie?" I repeated.

Ida turned from me to Brenda. "You've got to get Carrie away from your baby."

"Why?" she asked as the horror of it hit her.

I moaned. Not Carrie. "Carrie would never...."

"Oh no? Aren't they rivals? Doesn't Carrie know about the marriage plans?" And then Ida said, "You're not the professional here, I am."

I wanted to go home and get numb. Have some more wine, smoke a joint, but Brenda insisted I follow her home were Carrie waited. She was babysitting Brenda's daughter. It was her summer job before college in the Fall.

Brenda ran from her car leaving the door open and dashed into the house. The baby danced a little jig at seeing her mother and Brenda gathered her up into her arms. She pointed at Carrie with her chin as she took the baby away. Carrie walked toward the front door from the back of the house, her eyes wide with surprise.

"Hi, Carrie," I said. She hadn't changed much in two years. Still tiny and pretty.

"I didn't expect to see you here."

"We need to talk. Let's go outside, okay?" I turned for the door.

"I have to get back soon. My boyfriend is picking me up."

"This won't take long. Let's go around the block." She followed reluctantly and we walked in silence until we reached the end of the tree-lined block well away from the house. "I've been with Brenda all afternoon. We went to Dr. Ida's together."

"You told her about Dad and me, didn't you!" She released a nervous giggle. "Boy! Dad's going to be mad at you!"

We were facing each other on the sidewalk. "He's already mad at me, Carrie."

We walked on, silently thinking about that. I took a deep breath and stared at my feet. "There are legal problems, Carrie."

"Legal problems?" She also looked down as we moved along.

"Brenda could lose the baby if she exposes her to your Dad, especially if she divorces Andy." I didn't tell her that we needed to get her away from the baby. "Come stay with me again!" I cried it out passionately but she shrugged and kept walking.

"I'm going to college," she replied, and I remembered that college for Carrie was not just an educational opportunity but a state of grace.

"In France last summer—" I stopped her by putting my hand on her shoulder, "Did he proposition you?"

She giggled again. "No, that's been over for a long time."

"Why do you laugh?" I was suddenly furious.

"I always do that," she said, doing it again.

"But it's so serious and this is a mask." I put my hand on her face to pull the smile down but when my fingertips touched her cheek, a shock shot through my hand up to my shoulder and I almost fell to the ground. Her face was not flesh but wood.

I steadied myself. My hand hurt. "If I find the best therapist who is a specialist on this, will you go to counseling?"

Her small mouth was set and drawn. I noticed that the sun was sinking and long afternoon shadows lay over us both as we stood under the trees. "I like you better this way, Carrie. You're real." There was no reply, only a lifting of the chin. "What if I go with you? We'll go together."

"I've lost the babysitting job, right?"

"Right."

"Okay, you find the best there is and I'll think about it." There was no giggle, only anger. "My boyfriend is here. I see his car."

I spent Thursday and Friday on the telephone calling rape hotlines and battered women's shelters. One name came up over and over. I also found that the famous therapist had written a book on incest. I drove to Sisterhood Bookstore in Westwood and bought it. I finished it over the weekend and on Monday I made an appointment.

I drove to the mid-Wilshire district. I was not to meet with the famous therapist herself but with her protege. I was to be screened. Her name was Deanna. I babbled. I had a cast of thousands with infinite complications and ramifications. I had to get it all in within the fifty minutes. I was awash in compassion for everyone, even Bri.

"But what about you?" she asked gently.

"What about me? What do you mean?" I tried to brush the question away. "Why does everybody ask me that?"

She settled herself comfortably. She was plump, rosy cheeked, with dyed strawberry blonde hair and carefully painted makeup. She was too Hollywood for me. I glared at her but she said, "They do?" She raised a perfectly plucked eyebrow.

"I'm okay," I said defensively. And then I giggled.

"What happened to you?" she said, not appearing to notice.

"My father played with my breasts! So what!"

There was part pity, part humor, part sadness displayed on her pink glossy lips. "You speak of everyone else but they are not your responsibility. What about you?"

"I'm here for Carrie."

"But she's not here, is she? You're here and you're in pain but you pretend you aren't." She sighed. "Instead you focus on everyone else. Your brothers, your sisters, your niece. Incest victims like you will do almost anything to get out of feeling their own pain."

"Well fuck," I replied grimly.

4

When I entered the waiting room, I found that the place was crowded with women who obviously knew each other. They laughed and cracked jokes and I huddled into one corner of a sofa in angry terror. One of the women separated herself from the faceless mob and sat down next to me. She was big and blonde and soft. "Your first time?"

Jesus Christ! I thought, it shows. I nodded stupidly, unable to speak.

"Hi, I'm Susana Martin." She put her hand out. "What group are you in?"

I shook her hand. "Deanna's."

"Oh, she took you for herself, did she? Good. You'll be in the same group with me, welcome." She beamed gently and just as I was feeling a little better she added, "Feeling bad now, huh? Don't worry it'll get worse, much worse."

All the other women in the room who had been listening to this exchange broke into boisterous, bitter laughter. "Ain't it the truth?" This woman had rushed into the waiting room with her dark hair falling down out of its knot. She hitched her briefcase up onto her hip. "You new? She's with us?" She looked at Susana for confirmation and then back to me and didn't pause,"I'm Kelly, and Susana's right, of course. God! Why do I come here? I must be nuts. Well, of course I am, that's why I'm here. What's your name?" She perched on the edge of the sofa arm because there was no place else to sit. But before I could respond to this breathless monologue, the famous therapist swept in and swept out again with her group in tow. The waiting room was suddenly half empty and I found myself with Susana and Kelly and another woman I hadn't noticed in the hubbub. She was small and dark, sitting gloomily on the far end of another sofa looking as though she spent most of her time in corners searching for spots on the floor.

"That's Marsha," Kelly said. "What's your name anyway? Oh, I talk too much." Kelly threw herself into Marsha's sofa and spread out, flinging her briefcase onto the coffee table.

"I'm Annie Malloy," I managed to insert, and Marsha nodded, returning to her study of the rug.

The door opened and a young red-haired woman, slight and pretty with a wasp waist and tiny high breasts entered saying,"Am I late? Is Deanna here yet?"

Another woman followed her, catching the door as it swung shut. She was fortyish, heavy-set, and short. "Not here yet, huh. Hi, she new?"She addressed this to the air.

Both women settled themselves and greeted Marsha. Susana took over the introductions. Melanie was the wasp waist and Elaine the heavyset one. Just as I was shrinking away from a thoughtful group inspection, Deanna opened the door for Christina, a startling woman in her late twenties. She was a model with blonde streaked hair and a perfectly matched costume of leg warmers, an off-the-shoulder sweatshirt and tights, all color coordinated in pastels of pink and grey. Even her tennis shoes were pink and grey and without a single smudge. Deanna studied us all with a proprietary air and spotted me. "You've met the group?"

"Some," I mumbled.

"Well, good. Let's go and I hope you folks have been quiet out here." She took us into the maze of therapy rooms, to a room with white couches forming a U. Deanna sat down in a highbacked office chair on a swivel. It was placed in the mouth of the U like a throne. I learned that she always sat there except when Kelly attempted one of her coups and had to be thrown out. The coffee table in the center supported a miniature gumball machine filled with red and purple gumballs. I immediately headed for a corner spot on the far end of one couch and Susana sat down next to me.

I became aware that there were turtles everywhere. Wooden turtles on bookcases, stuffed cloth turtles in every size and color on the floor and end tables, posters of turtles including the one which announces the necessity for sticking one's neck out, and a tiny crystal turtle which was to become my friend on the Tuesdays that lay ahead. A tiny crystal turtle which tumbled in my fingertips, and soon lay clutched in my palm, piercing my flesh with its miniature claws. Every Tuesday night I would pick the turtle up and every Tuesday night at nine-thirty or ten-thirty, when things were really hot and heavy, I would put it down and go home.

"Do we have to tell our stories?" Melanie's voice was suddenly high and squeaky.

"You know we do." Deanna settled herself comfortably into her chair. She explained to me, the newcomer, "When we have a new person we have initiation."

46

Melanie sat on her hands. Kelly muttered, "Oh no, not again!" Marsha studied the shoelaces on her running shoes. Susana got suddenly still and Christina allowed a frown to mar her perfect forehead. No one spoke and Deanna waited.

"Okay! Okay!" It was Elaine across the table from me. "I just know you want me to start. So I will. So there! Now how does this go again?"

Deanna raised her eyes to the ceiling. "You know very well how it goes, Elaine. You say your name, your age, when the incest started, and when and why did it stop, who did it and what they did."

"Fuck," Kelly muttered. Melanie blew her nose. I was paralyzed.

"Okay! Okay!" Elaine repeated and everybody laughed. Even me. "I'm getting pretty good at this actually," she said folding her hands over her ample belly. "I'm Elaine and I'm a housewife and I'm forty-three years old. I have three children." She sagged a little as she sighed. "The incest started when I was six years old as far as I know. Everybody did it to me. My whole family."

The laughter was gone. There was an intense listening. She seemed to be telling her story directly to me. It was during Elaine's story that I discovered my friend, the crystal turtle.

"My father inserted things into my vagina to stretch it: candles, carrots, bottles. At eleven, we started having intercourse."

I noticed that my knuckles had turned white from gripping the turtle so tightly. I opened my hand to see if I had broken anything but the turtle was intact. There were red marks on my palm.

"My mother gave me enemas every Saturday morning from age five to age fourteen and I have no idea why she stopped. My father stopped when I got my period. My two older brothers used to tie me up and put me in closets and things like that. I guess that stopped when I got big enough to fight back." Her voice was very tired and she looked to Deanna who nodded.

"That was good, Elaine. Clear and simple. Huh" She questioned the group who agreed with "Yes" and "Great." Deanna's gaze moved to Melanie who sat to the right of Elaine.

"Oh, do I have to?"

"Yeah."

Melanie turned toward where I was sitting on the next couch. "I'll see how this goes. The first eight weeks I was here, I cried through the whole thing and couldn't talk. Do I have my kleenex?" She searched around the table, her lap, the couch.

"Here," said Susana patiently, handing her the box. It had been on the floor at her feet.

She pulled out two tissues as the group waited. "It only happened once."

"Once?" Now I was really getting mixed up. It made sense why Elaine was here. Her story was horrible, much worse than mine, I had reassured myself. But now Melanie was talking.

"My Dad took me with him on a business trip. I was eleven and we stayed together in a motel room and he decided, he wanted. . . ." She started crying and Elaine stroked her shoulder, her hair. "He decided that he was going to teach me about sex and so he made me rub his penis with my hands and he came all over the sheets and my blouse and my fingers and my chin." Then she wept through wads of tissue supplied to her by Susana one at a time as she soaked them. When the storm passed, she raised her head and faced Deanna. "Pretty good, wouldn't you say?"

"Pretty good," Deanna agreed and signaled to Marsha who was still studying her shoelaces as far as I could tell.

She raised her head. She was quite pretty, I realized, but an aura of sadness encircled her. It made her delicate features ponderous, her dark eyes a study in sorrow. Flatly, in a

48

monotone, she reported, "My Dad came to my room. Oh, I'm Marsha and I'm a secretary. Anyway, he came into my room every night from when I was eight, I think, until I was eleven or twelve, I think, I can't remember. He came and sang lullabies to me and while he sang, he would touch my forehead." She touched her forehead reverently. "Then my face and mouth." She touched her face and mouth. "And then my breasts and then he put his hands in my panties." Her hand hovered above her breasts and genitals. She stopped.

Deanna urged, "And then?"

"He stroked my vagina." She stopped again.

"What did you do?" Deanna asked.

"I pretended I was asleep." There was surprise at the question, as if she were asking, What else could I do?

"Why did it stop?"

"I don't know," she replied and returned to her study of down there: rugs, spots, shoes.

It was Christina's turn. While I waited for her to begin, I wondered why my chest felt crushed under a ton of lead.

"This is my third week and I'm new, too!" She said it brightly and I could see she was upset about not being the baby anymore. Casually, she announced, "Well, I was raped by my parents' friend when I was twelve years old. I was babysitting his kids and one night he didn't take me home right away. It hurt a lot but I was so lonely. I let him do it. I thought he loved me. He said he did, and we did it a few times but then he dropped me. Just like that." Her perfect face crumbled into little pieces and lines and her bright voice faded away and came back again as a brittle splinter of sound. "And my Dad didn't believe me and why would he since he goes to prostitutes all the time." She paused and stared at me defiantly. "I always wondered what I would do if I ever saw him on one of my outcalls." And so I learned that Christina had been a hooker from age fourteen to twenty-two and that she had had a hard struggle to give it up.

49

Kelly was almost beside herself. She twitched and hitched at her hair until it all tumbled out of its confinement onto her shoulders. Then Deanna's sigh unleashed her. "Well, I found out something new I'd forgotten! I went to hypnotherapy and I remembered my father. . . ." Her enthusiasm collapsed. "Do I have to do this?"

"Yes," Deanna replied firmly.

"I'm Kelly. I'm thirty-four years old and I'm a management consultant with my own business. The incest was with my brother. When I was six years old, he raped me. He was thirteen. He raped me repeatedly for about one year and sometimes he invited his friends in, too. It stopped when my parents sent him away to military school." She sagged. All her inflated self-confidence had vanished.

"Your mother," Deanna prompted.

"My mother," Kelly repeated, never taking her eyes off Deanna's face as though Deanna could hold her up, keep her from drowning. "My mother abused me. She pushed me downstairs. She burned my fingers. She verbally abuses me to this day."

"The new thing?"

"My father, too," Kelly uttered gently. "When I was three, I had to suck him off to orgasm. No wonder I can't eat bananas without slicing them into very, very fine little pieces. I don't know why my father stopped. He kept his underwear in a chest of drawers in my room. There was no place for his clothes in their room because my mother had so many clothes."

I wondered if there was any air anywhere. There was a lead elephant sitting on me. I clutched the turtle. It was Susana next and then me. I wondered if I would live that long.

Susana's voice was as soft as the rest of her and when she started, a smile came into the room and breathing was suddenly easier. It was clear that an old, familiar, and much loved story was about to be told.

50

"I couldn't tell my story for a long time and I was stuck. I would just sit here and refuse to talk." She moved her big body toward me. She was about five-foot-ten and yet dainty, very feminine in a pastel blue dress, her silky blonde hair curling around her ears. "I live two hours from here and one night after group I was driving eighty to get home on the Two-ten Freeway. You know the Foothill Freeway?" I signaled that I did. "The California Highway Patrol stopped me." There were now expectant smiles everywhere,even on Marsha's face. "So I told him. It all came out in the dark of the night on the side of the freeway in one big rush. Everything. It took about fifteen minutes and he just listened."

"Did he give you a ticket, anyway?" I asked.

"Yes, yes, he did."

"What is the story?" Deanna inquired pointedly.

"Oh. Yeah. I'm Susana and I'm thirty-seven years old. I'm working on my Ph.D. in Anthropology. It was my grandfather. I had to kiss him whenever he wanted me to. He put his tongue in my mouth. It was huge. He called me his little girlfriend and I had to hold his hand in the car and pretend with him. Sometimes he put his hands down inside my panties. I think he did it to my mother as well. I think it stopped when I was eleven or twelve. He died around then. It started when I was seven."

The air all around me was frozen solid but Deanna's voice penetrated anyway. "Annie?"

"My name is Annie Grace Malloy," I whispered. "I'm forty-two years old and I'm a computer consultant." I thrashed around on the couch. I had completely forgotten what I was supposed to be doing.

"Incest," Deanna reminded me after a long pause. "When did it start?"

"When I was twelve," I replied meekly in a twelve-year-old voice. "My father would make me lie on the couch with him after dinner to watch television. He would stroke my breasts under my blouse and pinch my nipples. The whole family would be there watching TV while this went on." Everything was dark around me as I was transported back to that room with only the flickering images of the black and white television to light the way.

"Annie." Deanna's voice came through the ice wall again."Why did it stop?"

I returned to the here and now with a jerk of surprise. "My mother. She sent me away when I was fourteen, to Catholic boarding school." I watched my hands in my lap. I wasn't sure they were mine. They looked like my mother's hands.

"That was really great for your first time, Annie." Warmed by Deanna's approval, I risked raising my eyes but then she said, "Melanie, you like this part. You explain to Annie."

Melanie proudly announced, "And now the final step in initiation."

"What? There's more?" I was in a panic.

"You must stand in front of each member of the group and say: 'Now that you've heard my story, what do you think of me?' "

"You've got to be kidding!"

They weren't kidding. When I stood up in front of Susana, a fury rose up behind my outward humility. But the fury and the humility were at such odds with each other that I expended most of my energy in the simple act of standing. Something had me by the knees. I staggered from person to person asking that question: "Now that you've heard my story, what do you think of me?" They told me I was brave, strong, wonderful and good. But I didn't care. I was pissed.

* * * * *

The fifth or sixth Tuesday I came to group jaunty with defiance. Deanna asked, "Annie, please read your letter."

"I didn't write one," I replied stubbornly.

"Why not?"

"I didn't think it was that important," I said smugly.

Her voice took on a dangerous tone. "What is more important than this?"

"I don't know what you're talking about." I hated the bitch.

"Your life, I'm talking about your life. What is more important than cleaning up the mess your life is in?"

"In the first place," I proclaimed solemnly, "I didn't come here to work on myself. I came here because my niece needed help and you talked me into this group." I waited for her answer to that one.

"I know all your tricks, Annie Grace Malloy. You dash about saving everybody else so you won't have to look at yourself and your life. You can't save your niece. You can't save your sisters or your brothers or your mother or your father. You can save only yourself."

I went up in flames. "I thought I was done with all of this. I've kept my journal. I've done my homework. Where's my A? My A for effort?" And as I shouted this some small sane part of myself inquired mildly: *A? You think life is a test to be graded? An A for effort is handed out to failures.*

Deanna simply looked at me. I looked back at her, seeing her rosy skin, her strawberry blonde hair, her perfect valentine lips. She glowed on her throne. The group listened and watched intently and I perceived that they all knew something I didn't.

"All right!" I couldn't stop shouting. "Fix me! Just inject it into my veins." I exposed my vulnerable inner arms. "I want the quick fix, the crash course and I want it now!"

"Annie Malloy," she said quietly, "I've had it with you."

"Yeah?" I sneered.

She settled herself firmly into her chair and there was challenge in her eyes. "Guess what? I'm the boss here."

"The boss?"

"The boss. There's only one boss in this room and it's me, not you." She turned to Kelly. "And it's not Kelly either." Kelly laughed.

"The boss?" I repeated.

"Yes, Annie, the boss."

"You're sure?"

"Yes." She smiled a tiny smile.

"Thank God."

"Thank God?"

"You mean somebody's in charge?"

"Yes."

"And it's not me?" I asked her again just to be sure. "It's you?"

"That's right."

"Oh good," I whispered in relief.

"Your assignment for next week?" She arched an eyebrow.

"Yes," I replied meekly.

"Take some gumballs."

"Now?"

"Yes, that's right. A handful at least."

I pushed the lever. Red and purple gumballs tumbled into my grubby hands.

"You will write a letter to your aggressor while chewing gumballs and sitting on the floor."

The next morning, I clutched my gumballs wondering if it was really safe to be little, to be a child, even for a few minutes. Even if I was now forty-two years old and this was just a game. I wrote:

Dear Daddy,

When you put your hands on my breasts, I was afraid. My breasts were brand new. I had just grown them. Mother told me that I had to wear a bra all the time now after she saw Mr. Gibson looking at me in the grocery store.

When you put your hands on my breasts, I wondered if this was what Mother meant when she said, "Be nice to Daddy."

It didn't seem right though because when you stroked my breasts and my nipples got hard, Mother watched from the doorway and she was mad. I could tell by her face.

When you put your hands on my breasts and whispered those things about Mother into my ear, I didn't know what to do.

I was afraid to push your hands away because I was afraid you might hurt me. You might pinch me or poke me. I have watched you put rubber bands on the tails of kittens to hurt them.

Nobody comes to the rescue but me.

Annie

I was sitting on the floor having trouble with my gum. I had put all the balls in my mouth at once and now the wad was almost more than my jaw could handle. I decided to never mix red and purple again. When I read what I had written, I spit the wad into my hand and pressed my forehead down on the cool glass top of the coffee table. "Nobody comes to the rescue but me," I said aloud. There was cool glass between me and all my feelings but a memory came up sharp and clear:

I kicked Harold Blare in the balls. I kicked Harold Blare in the balls because I knew he loved me and because he loved me, I knew he couldn't hurt me. And I knew he loved me because he knew I had a passion for his rage, his rebellion. I kicked Harold Blare in the balls because he wasn't my brother Bri, and so I could get away with it. I kicked Harold in the balls because he was weaker than me on the inside where it counts. I kicked him because he and his toughs were storming the house and because I was a warrior defending my flock, my mob.

Mother and Daddy were gone for a day of baseball and drinking in another village far away. I was in charge. The village was empty of adults also gone to the baseball game. Harold and his gang were roaming the hills and lanes in boredom. I had a mob and he had a gang. He was thirteen and I was eleven. His gang was all male, all the same size but smaller than Harold, and all the same age. My mob was smaller than me too but they were all different sizes and ages. Bri was just ten and growing. Maggie was an eight-year-old version of Bri with her fierce red hair and freckles. Kathleen was an ash blonde beauty of six. DeeDee was four and wanted to be important. Kevin was two-and-a-half, and Stella not even a year.

Harold's gang had the advantages of experience in walking, talking, running, fighting. My mob had the rudiments of motor coordination and speech. His gang were all toilet trained. His gang roved the village. My mob was fortified and we had a siege mentality.

It would be difficult to determine which group was the more frightened and lonely.

Harold's error was attacking me in my fortress. His siege brought the mob in line behind me. I did not often accomplish this by myself. His siege heightened my protective ferocity. His siege gave me a rare opportunity to express my violence. If he had caught me alone in the wood, I would have had no choice, my physical inferiority would have left me open to his rape. Or, in gentler circumstances, he could have courted me and perhaps I would have surrendered to him. But he was afraid. My reading had already taken me beyond him, beyond the village, the golden wood, the lakes, the gentle hills. So Harold was afraid and he did not come alone.

And so I kicked Harold Blare in the balls because I couldn't kick Bri in the balls even though I wanted to because I could feel him growing. Getting bigger, long boned, taller, heavier than me. Bri was waiting impatiently for the inevitable day. I had to make my plan against Bri's assault. I had to make sure that he would never dare. Bri needed a demonstration.

Harold and his gang failed to get into the house through the windows on that silent Sunday afternoon because even after they had removed the screens from the windows, nobody had the nerve to break the glass. Tomorrow would have to be faced.

So Harold ran around the back of the house and I heard him and waited at the kitchen door. The mob was behind me in a lump of bodies all pressed together. I handed baby Stella to Maggie. Bri was to my right peeking over my shoulder. Harold opened the screen door into the enclosed porch which was cluttered with leftover mittens, galoshes, fishing rods, winter coats, broken toys, mushy baseballs. The screen door was hung with strips of newspaper and sticky fly tape and as Harold came through it, I crossed the porch and with unerring skill and a terrible joy, I kicked Harold Blare in the balls.

Emerging from my reverie with a start, I ran to the mirror in my bathroom and there she was, Annie Malloy at age eleven, as fresh as a wild tiger lily with her honey blonde

57

braids and a spray of freckles across the bridge of her nose spilling onto her cheeks. Her eleven-year-old skin and gray eyes. I shook my head and I was back. Forty-two with frizzed, permed hair cut short, and sad tired eyes. I threw my gum wad into the toilet and prepared for the workday ahead.

And next Tuesday night I presented the Dear Daddy letter to group. It never occurred to me to mention the memory although I could still feel the bite of my eleven-year-old rage in the back of my throat as I had gone through the intervening workdays.

Kelly snorted at my letter and refused to comment. Susana said it was a good beginning. Marsha announced to Deanna that I would surely have to write several father letters.

"What are you talking about?"

Deanna explained, "You will write these letters over and over until they are right."

"How will I know that?"

"You'll know. By the way, how did you fell about your letter?"

"Feel?"

"Yes, feel."

I shrugged. "I don't know. Not much."

"Make something up."

"Ah, well, I think my father is a bastard." I offered this politely hoping it would do. I hadn't a clue as to what she wanted from me.

More snickers and snorts from Kelly. Deanna gathered her with a glance. "You're still new and so I will let this go by. Let it be. Annie, for next week you are to write a letter to your mother." I slumped down in the couch thinking that she was done with me at last and then she added, "Did you sit on the floor and chew the gumballs?"

"Yes."

"Good. Do it again. Take some more."

"This is embarrassing," I muttered, pressing the lever. Christina read a letter she had written to her mother. It was interminable. I didn't understand any of it. Even Marsha said that Christina needed to write it over. Kelly defiantly read her fourth attempt at a letter to her mother and Deanna told her to abandon the whole thing and start over again with another father letter. Suddenly, I became aware that everyone was staring at me. I finally asked, "Why are you all looking at me funny?"

Deanna's calm and quiet voice wafted across the room through the haze of my perceptions, "What did you say?"

"What? I didn't say anything." I looked around in appeal but they all stared back. "Did I?"

"You said, " 'I'm queer.' "

Susana was sitting next to me again. "You did, Annie, just now."

"What were you thinking about when you said that?" Deanna asked. Then, seeing me prepare my defense, she added, "And don't say you don't know."

"Well, I am. I'm a lesbian. I don't know why I said queer." But I knew why. I was testing them all. I pretended that I wasn't examining every face with my highpowered bullshit detector.

Not one eyelash fluttered. Nobody turned away from me to hide her face. They all calmly waited. Stymied, I was reduced to stuttering, "Ah, um, I. . . ."

Deanna came kindly to my rescue. "Tell us what you were thinking about when you said that."

I was dizzy. What had happened to all those stock phrases: It makes no difference to me. Some of my best friends are gay. My brother is gay.

Nothing happened. They waited. "Okay," I said. "I'll give it a try." I sat up straight squaring my body so that I faced Deanna. I decided that I would pretend I wasn't the only lesbian in this group. "I remembered some photographs of my

59

mother and her two girlfriends. I think they were taken in nineteen thirty-five or so when she was seventeen or eighteen. They were all so young and beautiful. They were playing pirates on a sailboat and somehow they had rigged up a plank. They wore scarves around their heads and knives between their teeth and my mother had a black eye patch." I paused.

"And?" Deanna asked pointedly.

"Oh! Now I remember. It was your letter, Christina. The part about your mother keeping secrets." Christina's facial muscles tightened in acknowledgment. "My mother has never shared these photos with me. I saw them two years ago by accident but my sister Kathleen says she's seen them many times."

Kelly interjected, "Is there a point to all of this?"

"There are pictures of my mother kissing her girlfriends. Draping her arms around them. The pictures are every lesbian's pirate fantasy."

"Every lesbian?" Kelly queried. "So?" She challenged.

"Back off, Kelly. Annie, I want you to write your letter to your mother just as I told you." Deanna had apparently spotted my puzzlement because she added, "And think about your mother and secrets."

It was midnight when I got home but I couldn't sleep. I sat down at the brass, glass-topped coffee table. I sorted out my gumballs. Three purples, two reds and four greens. I put all four greens into my mouth. The hard candy shell was disgustingly sweet. Kid sugar. I opened my journal, picked up my pen and realized that I was about to write on a page already filled. It was titled:

The Lady

She is gracious, calm, lovely, kind—and the chatelaine of her castle. She is a gourmet cook, a potter and a good mother. She has a husband with a brilliant career. She has planned her life carefully and everything around her runs smoothly. We all count on her as sailors count on the north star. As the middle sister, she is our lodestar. Her life appears to march with stately grace across time as predictably as the changing canopy of the night sky.

This was written in a neat, steady hand clearly legible, the words marching evenly across the thick white unlined paper. I turned the page and the handwriting changed; it now sprawled in incoherent spirals. I peered closely.

She's so perfect. She drives me absolutely batshit.

And yet when I had accused her of not caring about me because I was a lesbian, she got on the next plane and flew to Los Angeles from Las Vegas just to see me. And it was Kathleen who had shown me the lesbian pirate pictures of Mother and her friends and it was Kathleen who fixed it with Mother when I dragged Laura with me to our one and only family reunion. All the family reunion photographs took place in Kathleen's back yard in Boulder City. When the spouse shots were taken, Laura stood next to me along with the wives and husbands.

Never mind that Laura and I had fought like banshees all the way from Venice to Boulder City in the searing desert heat. We wailed and picked. We yelled and sulked. "What are we fighting about?" I screamed.

"I don't know," she screamed back and started crying into her crab and avocado sandwich as we sat at a picnic table in a rest stop by the side of the highway. "I just know they'll hate me," she sniffled.

"Honey, they won't hate you." But I was not altogether sure of my own welcome.

When we got there, Kathleen informed me that she had already had "the talk" with Mother. "Just don't push it and don't bring up religion."

I translated for Laura later in the tent in the back yard. The tent had been my idea. We didn't have the money for a hotel and the tent meant that we could sleep together in privacy. "In other words don't talk about it and us."

"Oh good," said Laura ironically, "you mean that everybody knows but nobody says anything. Nothing like having a glass door on this closet we're in."

"Yeah, but it's not bad for the first time out with my family is it?"

"No," she admitted.

"And Kathleen did it for us."

She allowed that she liked Kathleen.

And so we went through family reunion rituals which turned out to be mostly about food with picnics and dinners. We stopped at my mother's apartment just as we were driving out of town. She was very polite. She served us homemade chocolate chip cookies and Lipton tea with milk. I was slavishly grateful and yet I detected an air about my mother. As if she had unexpectedly discovered a dead mouse in her purse and was still trying to figure out what to do about it.

But this was not getting my mother letter written and so I paged through my journal to the next thick empty white page.

Dear Mother,

Writing to you about incest is the final irony since you don't like me writing anything at all.

I don't need to protect you anymore. You seem to be able to take care of yourself just fine, you bitch. You have been taking care of yourself at my expense for a long time and now the free ride is over.

You want me to be a lesbian because then you don't have to compete with me for men. You even competed with me for the attention of shoe salesmen when we went shopping to buy shoes for me. There was the time you bragged that you had twenty-twenty vision when I had to get glasses at age fifteen. You never, ever told me that I was pretty. I hate you.

Annie

When I read this letter the next Tuesday night, Marsha suddenly woke up and announced that she didn't believe a word of it. "What happened to your worrying about secrets?" she wanted to know.

Christina jumped on me too saying, "Are you a lesbian because your mother wants you to be?"

I wanted to retort, *are you a whore because your father wants you to be?* Instead, I indignantly answered, "Of course not!"

"Wait! Wait! Wait!" Deanna commanded. "One at a time. Marsha, what do you mean you don't believe it? What don't you believe?"

"I don't believe she hates her mother. I think she wrote this letter just to please us. Not because it's real to her." Marsha's dark olive skin was flushed with this unusual effort.

I was on the edge of the sofa ready to defend my letter and myself but Deanna waved me back. She leaned forward toward Marsha with great intensity. "And why did she write the letter the way she did?"

Marsha panted like a little cat with a pink tongue. "She was being a good girl. Just for us." She smiled inwardly knowing that she had gotten it right.

And Deanna affirmed her. "Right, that's right."

Kelly was snickering in the background and I planned my revenge. I would get her when she read one of her letters.

Deanna was gazing at me. Then she asked me the question which was to plague me for the next twenty-three Tuesdays: "What, Annie, do you want from your mother?"

63

As I drove away into the dark and rainflooded streets toward my shabby rented house on the beach, I had a fleeting vision of myself kneeling before a statue in a cathedral. Cold and humble, the eternal supplicant. That old sentence from my journals came back to haunt me: "I seek the goddess endlessly but I cannot find her." Or perhaps that was my mother at the railing in front of the Blessed Virgin lighting endless candles in endless novenas in her eternal quest for heaven.

Once, I had worshiped her like the sun. I basked in her radiance, her glance, her touch, her word. And then her inner light dimmed and it seemed that I was still waiting for it to come back.

I knew what I wanted after Laura left me. I wanted warmth. I wanted to be held. I wanted my Mother to comfort me, but when I arrived she served me tea with milk and jello with bananas and I knew that I could not speak and that she would never forgive my tears. I wanted to make myself small so that I could cuddle close to her and she would not push me away saying, "That hurts. You know how my arthritis is." So small, so inconspicuous like a mouse in the wall catching crumbs as they fell unheeded. Stray beams of warmth and light unnoticed and not grudged.

Instead we chatted. She told me that she had attended her fortieth class reunion last May. I was riveted but I knew her well enough not to show it. Casually I asked, "How was it?"

"Well, there were eleven of us there. Two others had died and only one had come from further away than I did," she said smugly. "She was from Virginia." She put the kettle back on the burner.

"That's nice," I encouraged.

"The women treated me just like I was one of them. They said that if it had happened today, I would have graduated."

"Really? They said that?" I was so surprised that my voice veered out of control betraying my excitement. I squelched it and she didn't seem to notice. Something inside me, that which had been waiting, jerked a little and released like a freight car uncoupling itself and then moving away slowly, the movement so slow as to be imperceptible but inevitable because of the sheer weight and size of the thing. And in that release, I thought: "I've done it for you, Mother. I've done it."

She had not graduated from college because she had been expelled for being pregnant with me. Prospective teachers were not allowed to be pregnant in those days even if there was a hasty marriage to make it all respectable. My middle-class mother had married her Wisconsin farm boy. She even converted to Catholicism for him but my father was never able to adequately support his growing family and my mother's failure to obtain her college degree condemned us all to decades of poverty.

Now I understood why I had thrown myself into the Women's Movement as though I were drowning. Why I had subjected myself to so much confrontation and rejection by becoming a leader. Why I had become a general in the sex war. And now Laura had left me and the University was about to fire me because I could no longer tolerate the ambiguities in my position as a Women's Center director. I had realized it was over when one of the assistant vice chancellors showed up with a female physician from Tunisia dressed in a flowing sari. There was a red dot in the center of her forehead. The Vice-Chancellor introduced her by saying, "Dr. Abu Sa performs clitorectomies."

He stared brightly into my face. I was speechless with pain. My days were numbered. I had seen too much. The sexual harassment of women professors. The beaten women in our CR groups at the Women's Center. And then Laura left me to go to San Francisco. To be with other women. To get away from me who was crushing her with my need to have some control somewhere.

So I had lost Laura and the only job I thought I had ever wanted—teaching at the university and running a women's center.

But my Mother's apparently superficial chatter revealed that it had all been for something. I was free. I had paid my debt. I wanted to shout it out to her: *Mother! Mother! I did it for you, Mother. I've carried your banner all these years in atonement, in your war. I'm forty now, Mother, and I lay it down. Annie Grace Malloy, retired. Now, my life. My turn.*

5

For the next Tuesday night I wrote: Dear Annie; Dearest Little Annie; Dear Little Orphan Annie; and finally settled on Dear Child.

Dear Child:
Who are you? I can't remember much about you. I don't even like thinking about you because it feels grimy, dirty and old.
What a little drudge you were with all your duties. Washing, ironing, dishes, sweeping, mopping, peeling potatoes, changing diapers, wiping noses, holding babies.

Watching out for Mother and her fast hand and Daddy and his fast hands and hoping that nobody would spill their milk at supper time.

Let's go and read, read, read and forget all this. Pretend that none of this ever happened.

Annie

Elaine shifted her heavy body over the couch cushions until she was well on the edge. "Are you going to let her get away with this one, Deanna?"

Deanna put her fingertips together in a steeple. "What would you suggest?"

"I think she needs to write that letter you had us do a while back. The one that starts 'When I feel criticized. . . .'" Elaine was examining my face minutely. I was uncomfortable and rebellious.

"Why is that?" Deanna inquired mildly.

"Because I think she's hiding out."

"From what?"

"Feelings!" Kelly bellowed triumphantly.

But I was glaring at Elaine. "What gives you the right to give me an assignment? You're not the therapist."

"The right?" She smiled bitterly and relaxed back into the couch. "My one hundred new pounds which I gained in ten months. I know all about hiding out. More than you will ever understand."

I was bewildered. "One hundred pounds, but I thought. . . ."

"I know," she said sadly, "you thought this is just the way I am. But I gained all this weight after my brother raped his daughter and went to jail for it. It brought it all back to me. What had happened to me."

For the first time, I saw something beside myself in the group. I saw the true kindliness in Elaine's face. I acquiesced. "Okay, I'll do it."

The following Tuesday night I presented my letter and I read it directly to Elaine.

When I feel criticized it feels as though I have been strip-searched like a criminal. I am about to be sent off to jail. Anyone has the right to poke, probe, uncover and hurt me. I am helpless. Sometimes I think that if I am very, very still and show nothing, I will be safe. Sometimes I just start fighting frantically like a caged beast. I attack with my words.

When I was little I found a fairytale by Oscar Wilde about a sparrow who presses its breast to the thorn of a white rose so that a lover could give a red rose to his love. Then she tosses it away carelessly. I identify with the sacrifice of the sparrow. That's life. It hurts and I will learn to be that noble. I will expose myself. No, I will be exposed since I have no right to protect myself or no right to even survive and I will die nobly like the sparrow or the blessed martyrs.

Needless to say, if I screw up at the bank, I feel guilty all day. Owing back taxes is proof of my essential badness. When I am criticized, I know that I am bad. No good. Worthless. A worm beneath contempt. A target.

When I finished, there was an expanded silence. Elaine was flushed and smiling. She nodded at me. Deanna's calm voice pronounced, "You feel humiliated, don't you?" And, for the first time, I cried. Deanna rose from her high-backed chair and came to me on the other side of the room. She held me as I wept. Finally she said, "Sit on the floor." I fumbled questioningly. "That's right. Right there." I spent the rest of the evening curled at her feet looking up and feeling protected by her and Elaine and Susana and even Kelly. "Next week," she said, stroking my hair, "I want you to write a letter that starts with, 'If I were real.' "

I took gumballs without her having to command me and I drove home tired but refreshed, and relieved.

If I were real, I would have more fun. I wouldn't be alone so much because people would come over and play with me. They would bring me toys and I would have toys for them. I wouldn't be so serious like I usually am and I wouldn't have to talk as much. I wouldn't have to make up stories about everything just to entertain. I would just think that people liked me. I wouldn't have to work so hard at being liked or covering up when I am hurt.

If I were real, I wouldn't have to worry so much about everything and everybody. I mean, I worry about the Jews. I worry about little kids getting hurt and I worry about myself. Mostly I pretend that I don't because it's too scary to worry about myself too much. I mean about being lonely and feeling like I am bad all the time and being wrong all the time and whether or not Mother will approve of me.

It's horrible. I worry whether or not Daddy will be drunk when he gets home. I worry about Daddy and Mother yelling at each other.

If I were real, I wouldn't worry as much. If I were real, I wouldn't try to take care of everybody all of the time. The other kids don't like it; they call me "pushy." I just know that I'm the worst kid around.

I don't even know what's real. My favorite radio program was Let's Pretend. I bet if I were real I wouldn't read so much. I bet I would stop trying to have other people's lives instead of my own.

I bet I wouldn't be so afraid to feel stuff. I wouldn't be in hiding. I could come out and have fun.

I'd be prettier too. People say to me: "You're human after all." This is after they get to know me. After they see how I pretend to be tough.

What happened to me was so awful I just tried to pretend I wasn't alive. That my life was being lived somewhere else. In a book. Awful things happened to other people but not to me. Deep down I knew that it was not true but what did it matter? Who could I tell? Who would believe me? So I looked away from me and left myself all alone, which is dumb. I mean, that's unreal. How can I not be with myself? Maybe that's it. If I were real, I could just be with myself as I am.

The If I Were Real essay was a resounding success. I thought I was on a roll. I read the words as I had written them, in a breathless torrent. I was directed to the floor once more and as I sat there being small and safe and looking up, I examined the strange sensations in my body. I held the crystal turtle up to my eye and asked, "What is this?"

The turtle answered, "I think you feel happy."

6

"What an improvement!" Deanna announced. Kelly smiled at me. "What's next, Kelly?"

"Father letter," Kelly answered at once without pausing. She took the pin out of her hair and it fell like a dark cape onto her shoulders.

"Father letter," Deanna confirmed.

I wrote that one at the kitchen table when I got home. I had forgotten to replenish my gumball supply.

Father,
    They tell me there are holes in my story about you.
    I feel like there are holes in me.

When you put your hands under my blouse in front of everybody, it made me feel like I was nobody. Less than nobody. Less than the television program. Less than a rat who could get away out of the house to the fields and woods.

When you did this to me in front of Mother it made me feel like dying because you were just using me to hurt her and I didn't want to hurt her but you didn't care.

I guess you thought I was just a pig for fattening, slaughtering, eating and using as you pleased. You made me feel like dying but I hid instead. I have been underground all of my life.

When you fondled my new breasts, my nipples, you destroyed my sexuality for years to come. You not only invaded my childhood but my future as an adult.

I went out and had sex with two hundred men looking for something but I didn't find it. Teased and stimulated by you, the only thing I could do was to not come and now I don't know how to stop defending myself. I don't know how to have an orgasm with a lover.

Annie

By the time I hit the third paragraph, I was whispering and choking. What was I doing telling these strangers my secrets? I whispered and choked and finally stopped talking altogether. Susana told me afterward that my face was white.

Kelly got up and squeezed herself between Susana's big soft body and me as I clenched the journal not speaking. "You can do this. I know you can. Finish reading it to us." She did not touch me but she was close.

When I had finished, Deanna asked, "What are you feeling right now?"

"I feel so guilty," I replied meekly, hanging my head.

73

"What do you feel guilty about?" It was Kelly stroking my cheek.

"Laura. How I hurt Laura." I couldn't raise my head. I would never raise my head again.

"What about her?" Kelly insisted.

"I withheld my orgasm from her. I didn't know how to be lovers with her. I told her she couldn't give me oral sex." I wanted to dive under the cushions.

"Why not?" Gentle Kelly. Relentless Kelly.

"Because I realized that oral sex sends me into a rage and the only way I can come is if I'm in a rage!" I snarled this defiantly into Kelly's ear. "I didn't want to give that to her. I tried to explain it to her but I don't think she understood. I wanted to protect her from my anger. It wasn't her fault. I wanted her to save me, to teach me, but she didn't know how." I ended up with my nose in Kelly's collarbone. She had her arms tight around me.

She murmured over and over, "Annie is a good girl. A good girl." But I couldn't cry, just sob like dry lightning strikes without rain.

When Kelly had released me Deanna asked, "What's going on with you, Kelly?"

I watched her curiously as I blew my nose. She pushed her body more solidly between Susana and me on the small sofa. We were three peas in a pod. It was soothing.

Her lower lip trembled. She combed her long hair with her slender fingers in an upward sweeping gesture. "I thought Bob would save me. Help me enjoy sex. Help me have a good time but. . . ."

"But?" Deanna asked.

"But it didn't happen," I finished for her. "The worst thing is that Laura thinks I didn't love her." And then I was off again and Kelly started up and we wept into each other's arms. Susana rolled her eyes to the ceiling and stooped for the tissue box on the floor. "Is that Chanel Number Five?" I

74

asked Kelly and then we were all laughing and crying and I saw tears in Susana's eyes too. She fed us tissue patiently.

Deanna took a long, luxurious breath. "Nobody can save you but you. Good sex comes from within. A perfect screw is not a cure for the incest trauma." She winked at me. "Or whatever."

"Two hundred men?" Kelly asked, looking at me speculatively.

Embarrassed, I shifted around in my seat which wasn't easy because I was so packed in. "The crazy thing is that Laura was upset about that too. I mean there were two hundred men and then her. I tried to tell her. Two hundred men weren't a match for her in my eyes." I glanced over at Christina who wouldn't look at me at all. I wondered if whoring was really the search for the perfect screw.

"It sounds like Laura let you be real for the first time in your life." Deanna said this slowly, thoughtfully.

"What?"

"Well, didn't you feel your real feelings about sex with her?"

Tears again and choking but I hung onto Kelly's hand which was in my own and her grip was as tight as mine. "Yes, but they are or were so negative. I. . ." And then waves of gratitude to Laura swept through my guilt and love followed behind that. "She let me say no to her even when it did not please her."

"That's a true gift." It was Christina speaking. You're lucky. Lucky to have had love like that."

"I am?"

"I think she's right, Annie." Deanna affirming this.

I took in the circle of faces around me. Susana, Kelly, even Marsha had roused herself out of her stupor and smiled in approval and acceptance. I decided later that it was almost as good as being cheered for marching in the Gay Parade in San Francisco.

75

When I got back to my new condominium in the Palisades, I ran the bath and lit scented candles. I lay back in the warm water and thought about Laura. *My Sweet Christian,* I called her. I was referring to her fundamentalist upbringing. She had been so shy about her body. It was my pleasure to act as her handmaiden when she soaked in the tub. I would be sure to be there when she rose out of the water. Her fair skin with the rose blush beneath and the golden tangle of curls at her thighs and her heavy breasts swinging gently as she moved. I handed her the big bath towel. I liked the orange one best; it suited her rosy golden coloring. She was a lioness. At first, she was shocked to find me naked in the tub with her but later we had our best talks there, our best kisses. Now, she stalked about her own rooms naked. Perhaps I had given her something after all.

Inspired by my self-congratulatory mood, I pulled the plug and wrapped myself in a white terry cloth robe and sat down at the kitchen table and wrote a letter to my Mother.

Dear Mother,

Now I feel ready to write this letter to you. I received your Halloween card and I found that I was avoiding you again. I sent you one back because I love you. That is a given and inescapable fact. I don't like you very much, though. I would like to change this so that we can have a better relationship.

I avoid you because you always talk about your sex life with me. Even when I was a child you told me about it. I don't like to hear about your sex life. It makes me uncomfortable and run over. I support you having a full and joyful sex life but I no longer wish you to share the details with me. I would really appreciate hearing an answer about this from you.

Love,
Annie

I bore this off to group next Tuesday night like a kitten bringing her first kill to her mother. "I want to send this one. I think it's simple, clear and good." I smiled smugly.

Kelly pounced. "Give me a break! What is all this love stuff?"

"Yeah!" Christina added belligerently.

Susana said, "I don't think you're ready to send anything." I could see that Deanna and everyone else agreed.

Melanie started crying. "My mother drives me up the wall, too. I know just what you're doing. You don't want to face it."

Deanna repeated her tedious question. "What do you want from your mother?"

"To stop talking to me about her sex life!" I shouted.

"Well, that's okay. That's good, in fact. But there's more, isn't there?"

I could see my lower lip. I refused to answer. I joined Marsha in looking down. I noticed that my running shoes were falling apart. Even the shoelaces were held together with knots.

"Annie?"

"What?"

"I want you to come in for a private session."

"Don't want to."

"Annie?"

"If you insist."

"I do insist."

"When?"

"Tomorrow at five."

I showed up in my office clothes. "Very nice," she commented, directing me to a white love seat.

I sat primly with hands folded and navy blue pumps lined up neatly with each other, knees pressed together. I pulled my skirt down. I adjusted the collar of my white silk blouse. "Well?"

77

"Well, where do you feel it?" she asked. She was wearing a pink silk dress and diamond studs in her ears. With her smooth skin and red hair, she was some sort of a human rose.

"Between my shoulder blades. Where else?" I felt navy blue and white all over.

"Will you take off your shoes and your blazer?" She asked so politely, I could not refuse her. She pulled cushions from the couches and piled them on the floor. She kicked off her own pink sandals and sank gracefully to the white carpeted floor. "Join me."

My back was suddenly naked under the thin silk of my blouse.

"Breathe!" she commanded. Then she touched me gently between the shoulder blades.

"Aaah!" It was a very little scream.

"What was that?"

"I've been stabbed in the back with a, with a. . . ."

"With a what?"

"A fork. No, a knife. No, a claw. I don't know. All of them." I sank into the pillows and tears seeped out, wetting a small corner of the pillow fabric. But the tears faded and I heard a growling sound. It rumbled deep in my throat.

"What was that?" she asked again.

"I want to be the claw." I said into the pillow corner.

"What?"

I rose up. "I want to be the claw. I want to tear things and growl. Is it okay?" I took my journal from the table and tore blank pages in half. It wasn't good enough. "Got any old magazines?"

She went to the waiting room and brought back a stack. I held *Vogue* close to my face and ripped it to shreds. I ripped another along the binding. The slick colored paper slipped and slid away from me but not one escaped. As I tore faster and faster, the growls boiled out of my throat and erupted into snarls. "More!" I demanded. She handed me *House Beautiful.* "Veils!" I shouted and snarled. "I am tearing away veils."

The white room was filling with paper. Deanna left the room again and again to keep me supplied. I growled and tore and threw paper into the air. Patches and swatches of oversized confetti. The growls turned to laughter and when we were knee deep in paper, I lay down and covered myself with it. My navy blue skirt was hitched up over my knees. My back was damp with sweat.

"It's like money," I said, idly tossing handfuls at the ceiling.

"Money?"

"Well, yes. A kind of energy. My energy."

"Our time is up, Annie. I'm sorry. This is important and I wish we could talk but I have another appointment."

"Our time is up!" I was flabbergasted. "How long have I been doing this?"

"For almost the whole hour."

"You're kidding!"

"No, I'm not. Here, help me with the wastebaskets."

We stuffed torn magazine pages into wastebaskets as fast as we could. As I crawled around I realized that I was still growling somewhere deep within. I wasn't done yet.

I gathered myself together as best I could. There were bits of paper in my hair. My blouse stuck to my back. I stumbled out of the office building and crept across the parking lot to my car. When I got home, I kicked off my pumps and threw my purse onto the coffee table. I shrugged out of my blazer and stalked around my condominium in a funk.

I came to the family wall. I called it that because it was where I had hung the family reunion photographs and snapshots of my mother and me. I stopped dead in my stocking-footed tracks. I pulled the framed photographs of Lily and me off the wall, leaving faint lines on the white plaster. I took them all into the kitchen.

I went back into my bedroom and burrowed through the drawers in the closet where unframed piles of photos had lain quietly forgotten until now. I brought the ones of Lily and me together and threw them on the stack on the kitchen table.

I sat down. My back was cold and wet. I didn't care.

I took the photos out of their frames. I carefully put the silver frames to one side and then I methodically tore every photograph of Mother and me in half. When I was finished, I went back to the closet and got the large manila envelope I had spotted earlier. I put all the torn pieces into it and sealed the envelope shut. I took it downstairs through the garage to the trash can outside.

When I got back upstairs to the kitchen, I realized that the bottom of my white nylon stockings were filthy. I didn't care. I sat down at the table and with colored pens drew two bloody eyes with a grey veil over them. There was an impossible blue life force behind the blood in the eyes. Then I drew great zig-zagging lines across the whole image. At the bottom I wrote: "Ripping Open the Lie."

Exhaustion hit me suddenly and I went to my bedroom and fell across my bed. Guilt lay over me as palpable as smoke in a fire. I pressed myself into the bed as hard as I could hoping there would be more oxygen closer to the floor.

I was afraid to look up. Guilt was bursting the walls. With my face pressed downward, I reached to the telephone on the nightstand. I dialed Deanna's home phone number. I had never used it before. Her machine answered and so I left a message. "I just tore up all the pictures of Mother and me. I threw them away. Is that okay?" Of course, there was no answer.

I couldn't sleep and so I got up again. I rearranged furniture until the sun rose. All the funny spots on the walls were now covered with other pictures. I removed my torn stockings and changed into my running clothes.

I was possessed with a maniacal energy. By the end of my three-mile run, I decided that I would fly to Las Vegas and rent a car and confront my mother. I would be back in town before group on Tuesday night. I'll show them, I thought.

I called Kathleen when I got back to the house. I told her only that I was flying in for a long weekend. "Just to visit. One of the nice things about money is the luxury to be impulsive."

"Perfect timing," she responded, "Mother and Stella are stopping by tonight, too. We're having a little cocktail party, so bring a dress, okay?"

"Okay." My next telephone call was to the airport and as I drove away I could hear my phone ringing. Probably Deanna, I decided, but it was too late to talk me out of anything now.

As I drove up in my rental car, Kathleen was waiting for me at the front door of her four-thousand-square-foot house. "You look like hell," she announced.

"I know," I replied. "I haven't been sleeping very well." I didn't tell her I hadn't slept at all. "I'd love to take a shower."

"Use the guest bathroom downstairs. Did you bring a dress for tonight?"

"I don't have a cocktail dress. I brought my black silk pants and a light blue blouse. Will that do?" I could see that she was worried. "I promise not to disgrace you, okay?"

"Okay." With that she turned away into the house and I trotted behind her with my luggage.

Lily showed up at seven. I had not seen her for more than two years, since the trip to Trinity Lakes. She was elegant in a black cocktail gown with pearls at her throat. She pulled me into Mitch and Kathleen's bedroom and we lay together on their king-sized bed in near darkness as she launched into one of her stories about her sex life. "I had to get a padded headboard for my bed," she giggled. "The next-door neighbor complained." She did not ask me about myself. She did not comment on my puffy eyes or my dead white skin or my obvious distress. She did not inquire about my sudden appearance at Kathleen's cocktail party.

And I reverted to what I always was with her at these times. I became ear. I became funnel. I became that shape or function she desired. My chest was encased in steel bands and my ribs had turned to stone. Kathleen came into the room saying, "Shame on you two. Help me with the guests. Everybody's coming in now." I needed help to stand but I had to do it myself. Lily gaily bounced up from the bed and straightened her dress.

"Annie, we'll get to talk more this weekend at my place." And then she was gone into the lighted doorway where the party waited. I followed. Kathleen was moving from guest to guest.

I went through the motions of being alive and well. Kathleen came to sit by me during a lull and I put my hand on her arm. The flames flickered in the fireplace. "Kathleen," I whispered, "I'm so angry with Mother. Does it show? I can't breathe."

She looked at me in surprise. In her steady calm manner she said, "No, you look okay to me. A little tired."

"That's a relief. Just telling you helps." I didn't tell her that I was wondering how I would get through the night. I didn't have any asthma medication with me. I hadn't needed it for years. Maybe it would just be a small attack. Later, I fell asleep with my chest in constricted pain.

The next morning I went to Stella's house to help her prepare for a small dinner party she was giving to celebrate the purchase of her first house. "Do you and Kathleen always give parties the same week?"

"No. It just worked out that way for some reason. This is lots smaller. Kathleen and Mitch and the kids. Now you and Mother, of course, and her latest boyfriend and me and Jersey. No big deal."

I could see that it was a very big deal. Stella did not entertain often. We had an hour for ourselves because Jersey was napping. We prepared vegetables for the salad. Stella started on the mushrooms and I washed lettuce in the sink.

"I'm feeling really angry with Mother. I think it's part of my therapy. What should I do? Should I talk to her about it?"

Stella did not reply. She lined up mushrooms on a cutting board.

"Does Mother talk to you about her sex life? I mean the woman has a better sex life than I do and she's sixty-five years old, for God's sake. Is that fair?"

Stella viciously decapitated a mushroom and the sound of the knife hitting the board brought me back to the sound of a wooden door hitting a wall on a summer's day when I was nineteen and Stella was nine. I had opened the door. It was a door to the shed in the garden. There were flowers in the garden. Gladioli and pansies, snapdragons and sweet peas. Stella lay on her back on the bench in the warm shed. Her panties were down and she was alone. I backed out of the door into the flower-drenched sunshine leaving her to the warm darkness. I never told because I knew about the touching of that tight skin over the clitoris bursting like a bud through the soft damp folds of the pink vulva. A little girl's vulva. Hairless and pink like the petals of a rose.

I was pulled out of my remembrance by Stella saying sadly, "I can't even masturbate anymore."

"What?"

"I can't even masturbate anymore."

"Oh." I was slicing carrots now and trying to catch up. "What am I going to do about Mother? I have to do something. I almost had an asthma attack last night. I always thought Dad gave me asthma and now I think it was her. I don't want to be sick. It's not worth it."

"Sometimes I think I'll get cancer," she replied, washing cherry tomatoes one by one under the cold water rushing from the faucet.

She scared me. "If you think it, then you will. Don't let them kill you, Stella." I didn't mean "them." I meant Mother but I was too craven to say so.

She did not respond but set two wine glasses at the kitchen table. She went to the refrigerator and brought out a bottle of Andre's Cold Duck.

"I thought you stopped."

"I started again since the incest thing." She sat down and lit a cigarette. We had finished the salad. She waited for me to judge her but I just looked at her saying nothing. "I just do it at night after Jersey's asleep. I can handle it. He doesn't know." She inhaled deeply. "I have trouble urinating too." Her tone was clinical, detached.

"You do?" I was wondering if I were my sister's keeper. I picked up my wine glass and sipped. It was perfectly awful.

She relaxed and drank deeply. "Oh Bri used to make me touch myself on my clitoris and my urethra and sometimes he even made me pee on him. He used to lay in wait for me and catch me in the bathroom." She stopped in the middle of this revelation and turned toward the back of the house. "Shit! The kid's awake already and I've still got stuff to do. Will you?"

"Of course, you do your thing. I'll go see how he is." I could hear him crying that sleepy cry small children make when they wake up cranky from a nap. I went into his room and he wasn't there. His tiny bed was neatly tucked with a bright yellow quilt. I followed his snuffles and cries and found him in Stella's bedroom sliding down one side of the large mussed bed covers. I caught him as he fell and set him on his feet. He stopped crying and looked me over solemnly.

I lay back on the bed and as I lay back, I felt an overwhelming seductive force so strong it filled up the room in seconds. It was a rapidly expanding burst of the sweetest perfume. It was a yearning. Part sexual, part loving, part. . . .

Then I realized that it was emanating from the boy, my nephew, Jersey. He clambered up the side of the bed and I pulled him to me. He was completely silent now and watchful. I had not really looked at him before. I had only experienced him as a nuisance who clattered about my sister like a whirling dervish preventing contact with her. I picked him up and held him in the air above me and we played bed and baby games up and down. He cuddled himself up to me finally and went back into a light sleep. He had silky brown eyelashes and white pale skin with a touch of creamy brown beneath.

The dinner was almost ready. Jersey was screaming because Stella wanted to talk to me. In retaliation he got his toy train which ran on musical tracks. He was barely past three but he knew that the tracks make terrible noises when they are out of order and do not play a song. I realized that Stella was being held prisoner by her child.

Stella was beside herself. She was not proud of her small house when she placed it next to Kathleen's palace and the nicer Kathleen was, the worse she felt. "They think I'm low class. Especially her daughters. I just know it." She fussed with the ham.

I wanted to hang myself on the wall like a moose head and watch but it was too late. Mother was there with her latest man. He was a handsome and somber seventy in a three-piece suit. We had been warned to be on our best behavior. I wondered if he could get it up or was this the other one?

We all sat down at the long, linen-covered table and Lily abruptly stated the blessing: "Let us thank God, the Father, for these gifts which we are about to receive. Amen." We did or did not cross ourselves reflecting the various stages of our Catholicism. I did not, and my mother's cock worship suddenly had no bounds. It had never been so clear to me. I added to the blessing quickly, "And to the Goddess for bringing us together."

A tense gloom fell over the dinner table while ham slices, sweet potatoes, and salad were passed out. We heaped our plates as though we could cover my challenge with mashed potatoes. Halfway through my candied sweet potatoes I excused myself. I threw up into Stella's chocolate porcelain toilet. I understood that I had two choices. I could be sick or I could kill her. Neither was acceptable. I was stuck. I would have to speak.

On Saturday morning, I called Maggie. "What should I do? I'm so angry it's making me sick."

"I think you should talk to her. It will be okay."

Kathleen said only, "You have to do what you have to do." DeeDee refused to discuss it. Stella was noncommittal.

As I drove to my Mother's apartment on the other side of the city, I realized that for the first time in my life, she was safe. She had a studio apartment in senior citizen housing. She had an income. She was in good health.

She immediately took me on a tour of her small place. She showed me her new rug and her love birds in their cage in the kitchen. I examined the new blanket she was laboriously quilting. When she showed me the cushioned headboard, I opened my mouth to speak but she was too quick for me. "He always asks afterward if I feel guilty like other women do but I always say no." She laughed at that and showed me the sliding glass doors in the kitchen. "They're great for plants but I just found out that the neighbors can see in and here I've been wandering around nude."

"I've got to talk to you." It just burst out.

"Well, let me make tea first," she answered. It took her forever.

"I've been avoiding you for months. Since I started therapy."

She sat in her chair with the doilies and the footstool and waited, saying nothing.

I plunged in. "I find that I am very angry with you." There was cold terror all around me and still she did not speak. It was her Arctic silence.

I thrashed onward. "I'm not twelve anymore and you're not thirty-five. We are not the same people at all. I'm not trying to blame you. I'm not asking you to defend yourself but I must speak or I will not be able to be around you at all."

Her rocking recliner remained still. "Angry?"

"Yes," I said with relief. "I'm all mixed up. You see, I forgave you long ago but I never permitted myself to be angry with you. You and Dad are such opposites. He's such an obvious asshole. It's easy to be mad at him and not to see I could love him too. You know what I mean?"

Her lips were thin and grim. Her teacup froze in her fingers. "What are you talking about?"

"Why didn't you protect me?" It came out in a wail, a desperate cry. I instantly apologized. "Oh, I'm sorry that was my twelve-year-old talking." I squelched her savagely and in a calm adult tone added, "Dad molested me."

"I never knew that." The lines of her face became angles. Her lips white. She was wearing her granite face.

"I'm not twelve anymore!" But I was. In my heart I was. I had stopped there. I knelt in front of her, pleading. "But you saw! He did it in front of you on the couch after dinner. In front of the TV!"

"I never knew." She set her mouth around the pronouncement and I knew that she would not waver.

"But that's why you wanted to get rid of me. Throw me out of the house!" I flung it at her. Into her face. "Why did you compete with me?"

That roused her indignation. "I never competed with you."

"Yes, you did and why not? The man was a pig! Look what he did. He ended up with a woman only a few years older than me. I never blamed you. It was so awful in those days. All those babies one after the other and your cancer. I did everything I could for you now I need to have my life back. Please!"

She was grimmer and grimmer, like a sky suffocated with thunderclouds. She had taught me so well. How to flail and suffer in front of her while she remained impervious like some graven image of a goddess on a hillside far above me.

"This is all through our family. It's not just me, Mother." I got up and sat down again. "Thank you for letting me speak, I'm trying so hard to understand but I just had to say something. Thank you for letting me talk. I'm sorry if I hurt you." I went to her and bent over to hug her. "I love you, Mother."

She pushed me away. "No, you don't. You hate me."

She was only half right. I hated her and I loved her. "Oh no, no. Please. Please try to understand. I need to go on. We need to go on." I hugged her again but her body did not relent under my arms, my hands.

I ran out of the apartment to the car and returned to Stella's house. Nobody was home. This wasn't working out the way I wanted it. Somehow, I still wasn't done. I went to the refrigerator to find the Cold Duck but it was gone. Stella had finished it off. I was contemplating one of my hangnails when the phone rang.

It was Kathleen. "Mother is very upset with you, Annie."

"She is?"

"Yes. You know, Annie, Mother did the best she could under the circumstances. Isn't that all we can ask of anyone? The best they can do?"

"I suppose so," I agreed reluctantly.

"I'll pick you up in about an hour. Stella's going to meet us there. We still have to go through the photographs for

Maggie's birthday trip. Maybe we can get this all taken care of then."

On my way back to the apartment I kept thinking that my Mother was my own personal, private Medussa. If I could face her, I could face anything.

When we walked in the door, I knew instantly that my transgression had made the rounds. Stella was sitting on the couch as though she had been glued there. She would remain there throughout the fight, watching like a spectator at a tennis match. Watching her two mothers. Only her eyes moved.

Lily was in her recliner, her throne. I walked to the bedroom and threw my coat onto the bed. As I turned to go back into the living room, I found that my arms were swinging back and forth. I was looking forward to the fight. "Kathleen tells me that you are upset with me," I announced. "So let's have it."

"Yes, that's right."

Both the Frail Mother and the Dragon Mother had responded. I wondered how she managed that. It was quite a trick. I snorted at her.

She got up out of her chair and went into her narrow little kitchen and whirled around, rushing from that space like a dragon rising from her den and exploding out of the mouth of her cave into the bigger space of the living room.

I faced her waiting on the balls of my feet in the center of the room. Kathleen reeled about as though she were suspended on the sheer force of the tension between the Dragon and me. I was glad she was there. Her presence would prevent mayhem.

"What is this?" she roared. "Telling strangers our family business! Are you using our real names? I suppose you're writing this all down too, aren't you? Well, aren't you?"

The telling of the incest! The speaking of it. Of course, that's what would infuriate her. Not the incest itself.

89

Suddenly I was with my littlest brother Kevin at the family reunion. I understood him at last. He had wanted our father to attend the reunion, which was ludicrous considering that the man had left us all for another woman and the three children he had had by her in a secret ten-year relationship. But Kevin did not want his father. What he wanted was his image in the photographs. Evidence that we were a real family with a mother, a father and children.

"I've been waiting for you to die," I said quietly, to my mother. "So that I could write."

She didn't flinch. "So what's wrong with dying?"

"Well, I'm not waiting. I will not sit around and wait for you to die. I'm going to write and speak and you are not going to stop me."

Her nostrils were white. We circled each other like fighters in a ring. We were bounded by the couch on one side, the recliner on another, the windows and front door on the wall opposite the recliner, the mirrored closet door on the fourth wall facing the couch. She moved to the mirrored door. This was where she stored her treasures. Her photographs and mementoes. I followed. Her shoulders were hunched. We were nose to nose, eyeball to eyeball. I stifled the desire to laugh. I could see the pores in her skin. They were just like my own. Our noses were almost touching now and she said, "After all I've done for you."

I didn't waver by a nostril hair. I had survived ambush by pity. I had looked a dragon in the eye and lived. I loved her completely in that moment. As a warrior loves a worthy opponent. "And," I paused for effect, savoring it, "after all I've done for you."

She didn't move. Her jaw tightened. We hung there joined in the truth of the past and of how she had leaned on me crushing me with her needs. A grudging respect glimmered in her eyes. She appreciated power. She was stopped and she knew it. "Umph," she grumbled and straightened up.

90

As she moved up, the air cleared. Smoke drifted away. It was easier to breathe. She assumed her position in the recliner. I sat on the floor at her feet cross-legged, loose-limbed. I was ready.

She opened with, "You can't take my children away from me."

There was an eerie logic to this but it escaped me. I glanced at Stella and Kathleen in bewilderment, but they were only relieved that the physical confrontation had passed. My heart knew the answer but I didn't want to hear it. *My heart asked in its quiet way, aren't I your child, too? But I did not speak this aloud.*

"Just don't analyze me." Her voice was low and pleading. She addressed Stella and Kathleen. "The minute she popped out, she was analyzing me." She shook her head and spoke to me again. "I haven't understood you since you were six years old."

My child's heart shrank. *She's been angry with you since the day you were born. She hasn't forgiven you for something you did when you were six.*2 The adult part of me could not process what she was saying and promptly identified it as crazy, but another part of me caught on something. Smelled something, snagged it like a branch catching up a fish hook in a flowing river.

"Analyzing?" I said finally. I raised my eyes to her. "I've broken your code, haven't I?"

Now she had the stillness of the person who hears. "Yes, yes, you have."

"It's the code that says if you can't say anything good, don't say anything at all."

She nodded. "I told my mother I hated her once."

I snapped back, "Well, you were lucky if you had to say it only once."

Later Kathleen told me that Lily had never forgiven herself for this. Lily's mother had died the year I was born.

More than forty-two years had passed and she still carried the guilt.

Her guilt infected me and I faltered saying, "I'm sorry I broke your code but I believe the truth heals . . ." I trailed off, seeking help from Kathleen and Stella, but they averted their eyes.

Sensing my weakness she came back at me. "So you want me to accept this blabbing, do you? Telling strangers about us in your so-called therapy group. This writing everything down in your famous journals.

She drew herself up in her recliner, her throne. "What about your daughter? Why didn't you bring her to me?"

I was slammed. Stella squirmed in her seat on the couch and then I knew she had spilled the beans. Told Lily about me being pregnant at twenty-five and alone. I wondered if my daughter was one of the children I had taken away from her. It had never occurred to me to come to her for help. All I could say to my mother now was, "You have got to be kidding!"

"Well then, I guess we are even."

It made some sort of sense. I echoed her words. "We are even." There was bitterness running up and down my spine. I had lost my daughter. Given her up for adoption.

And then it was over as abruptly as it had begun.

Stella leaped up. "I want a cigarette. Annie why don't you come with me?" I followed her tiredly out the front door. We left Kathleen to put Mother back together so that we could select photographs for Maggie's fortieth birthday celebration coming up after Christmas.

I leaned on Stella even though I was five-foot-six to her five-foot-one. "Did I do okay?" I asked."

Stella smoked and marched briskly along in her high-heeled shoes and her short jacket with the sheepskin collar. I hooked my arm into hers. "Yeah." She was pleased that I would consult her.

"I feel pretty good but I slipped up a couple of times."

"Yeah, your child slipped out here and there but actually Mother's more of a child than you are."

I knew what she meant. I was accustomed to feeling like Lily's parent. "Thanks for being there."

"You're welcome. Those walls of hers. . . ."

I wondered where Stella was getting all of this psychological chatter until I remembered that she had been reading transactional analysis books.

"You kept throwing things at her," she said, "but she wouldn't let down." She paused and we watched our breath in the frosty air mingle with the tobacco smoke. "But if she did, she wouldn't have arthritis. . . ."

We walked awhile thinking about that and Lily's twisted hands.

Stella said, "She'd have to go to bed for two years."

This set us laughing. The very idea of Lily letting go.

We stopped abruptly. It wasn't funny. We took deep breaths and walked back. We were silenced by our own temerity. When we opened the door, we saw that Kathleen had done her work. They were sitting on the couch with a pot of tea and photograph albums spread out all around them.

7

I dragged myself back to group the following Tuesday.

"So did you tell her to stop talking to you about her sex life?" Susana asked this politely but her soft cheeks were flushed with anger.

"No," I admitted.

"And why not?" Melanie's lower lip was trembling. Susana handed her the tissue box automatically and she took it without looking.

"Well, I—I'm not sure. I just didn't get around to it I guess."

"You just didn't get around to it!" This was Kelly. Her hair was wild and snarled, falling around her ears.

"Why did you do it, Annie?" Elaine wanted to know.

94

"I was furious with her. I wanted to tell her, to get it over with."

"Is it over with, Annie?" Deanna's question.

"No, it didn't work the way I thought it would. I don't feel as angry as I did though." My teeth hurt. My jaw was sore. I had been chewing on nails.

"Don't do this again, Annie." Deanna drew herself up regally in her chair. You weren't ready. You will be. I promise. And then it will be important for you to confront your mother and your father but now you need to just be with yourself."

I sniffed.

Melanie added, "I called my mother after the first three weeks of therapy and now when I look back, I think it set me back months."

"Why?" I asked, not really wanting the answer.

"Because she crushed me and I wasn't strong enough to push back but I can tell that I will be soon. Not quite yet, but soon." She squared her thin little shoulders. "And I'm going to demand that they pay for my therapy, too."

"I want to know about your daughter, Annie. You have a daughter?" Christina's face was bright and open. I had never seen her that way.

"Yes," I said, "I have a daughter."

The old days of Jake and me and our affair. We went away together to Los Angeles. We lived in a two-room apartment near McArthur Park. I had started the pill which was still a novelty and I kept saying to my doctor, "I'm pregnant. I'm pregnant." And he would say, "No, no. It's just the pill." But of course I was right. The diaphragm had failed and by the time my suspicions were confirmed, I was four months into the pregnancy. Illegal abortions being extremely dangerous at that stage, I decided to have the baby.

I was stuck. Stuck with Jake and myself and my swelling body. He was furious with me for being pregnant but too guilty to leave and so he worked all day and played pool at night. He shouted at me if I complained of heartburn or the heat. He did not want to be seen with me in public. I was a secret. He didn't tell his parents about me and I didn't tell mine either. I was in hiding and I was lying as well. I tiptoed past the apartment manager's door every morning on my way to work because I knew that we would lose the apartment if they found out about me. At work I told everyone I was married. I used Jake's name.

My job astounded me. I had not known such regimentation before, not even at St. Katherine's High School with the nuns. I corrected the names, addresses and telephone numbers on computer lists of credit card customers. There were three hundred of us seated at desks in a large room. We were divided into sections and each section performed equally mind-deafening functions to keep the credit card machinery in motion. There were two hundred and seventy women and thirty men. The men were the supervisors. We lived by the bell. A bell rang in the morning and we started the day's work. Another bell rang for our morning break and each section rose up in order and marched upstairs for coffee. We were expected to be seated at our desks again before the bell rang signaling the end of our breaks. And so it went.

The women gave tupperware parties, sold Avon, bet on the football pool, and collected money from each other for weddings, funerals and other disasters. They gave me a baby shower. They didn't know that I had been reviewing resumes of prospective parents. That I had been making arrangements with the attorney and the doctor to give up my baby and that I had selected the parents on Tuesday.

There were diapers and safety pins with plastic yellow ducks on them and bibs with bears and blue and yellow blankets and pink ribbons and rattles and booties with lace trim. I took three shopping bags to the attorney's office and the ribbons and wrappings made a bright contrast to her leather chairs and law books. The lawyer said, "I'll give them to the parents. Are you sure you don't want to meet them?"

"No, no. I couldn't bear it." I ran away as fast as my heavy body could take me.

The company fired me when I was six months along but advised me that I would be allowed to come back if there was a job opening. The doctor gave me a slip indicating that I was perfectly healthy and able to work but no one would hire me and so I collected unemployment compensation. With nothing to do, I settled into the science fiction collection at the Los Angeles Public Library and finished it before the baby was born.

I called her Leslie. I knew she was a girl. She was born in the middle of the Watts Riots. The National Guard was in town with their tanks on the freeway overpasses. I collected my unemployment checks under gunpoint in downtown Los Angeles. It seemed fitting somehow.

"I wrote her a letter," I announced.

"Without being assigned to do it?" Deanna smiled at me. "Why don't you read it to us?"

Dearest Leslie,

That was the name I chose for you when you were in my womb. I hoped for a girl. I thought the name would make you strong.

I did the best I could for you. I hope you can understand. I tried to find the best parents for you. I'm sorry I couldn't bear to meet them. It just hurt too much. The letting go of you.

I remember your presence in my body very well. It was the oddest thing to not be alone in my body and when you were ready to be born, you kicked and squirmed. I heard you saying: "Let me out! There's not enough room in here!"

You came down the birth canal in three great shudders and I thought, There's a battering ram at the gate. But the drugs took me and when I woke, you were gone.

I asked to see you. It caused a big flap. The doctor had to write an order to make the nurses bring you to me. The nurse undressed you to show me that you were a girl. I held you for a few moments but I started crying and I couldn't stop. I cried for three days. They sent me home early because I just kept crying and they said that I was bothering the other mothers. It was the only time I ever saw you.

I think of you all the time especially on your birthday. I've been waiting until you are eighteen years old before I look for you.

I still believe I did the right thing. I have never doubted that. Your father was weak and incapable of caring for either you or me. I picked him because he was like my father. I wasn't very grown-up either. I tried to find a good mother and father for you. To give you the best chance. I hope it worked. I love you.

Your Birth Mother,
Annie Grace Malloy

"How old is she now?"

"She will be eighteen next year," I replied. "Why are you so interested in all of this, Christina?"

"I had a baby once. I gave her up five years ago. Will you look for Leslie?"

"Yes, I will."

"Let me know what happens, will you?"

"Okay."

"I want to know something!" Kelly fretted. "Weren't you mad at your sister Stella for telling your mother about the baby?"

98

I sighed. While it was true that I was accustomed to the deepest silence and secrecy about my daughter, it was also true that I was deathly sick and tired of my secrets. "I was relieved," I told her. "Relieved it was out. It was time for everything to be out and told."

"Oh."

"Deanna, I'll be seeing my family or at least my sisters again next month and I will go."

Deanna frowned at me. "What for?"

"It's Maggie's fortieth birthday and we've promised each other we'll get together every two years to celebrate each sister's fortieth. Mine was the first. We're going to Montana to ski."

Christina again, "Do you ski?"

"No, but I'm going to learn." I surveyed the circle of faces around me. "You're all from California, aren't you?"

"I'm from Chicago originally," Deanna corrected.

"Well, then maybe you'll understand. I have always been afraid of winter, of being locked inside with my family, I guess. I think I have terminal cabin fever."

"I'll bet there's a point to this somewhere," Kelly commented. Kelly was a true Californian, having been born in Van Nuys.

"Maybe I shouldn't have gone to Boulder City the way I did, but I learned something. I learned about my asthma. It was always worse in winter. It started when I was nine. I thought he gave it to me. But so did she! With her giggles and her chitchat and her pretending!" I was trembling now. "He had a history of pneumonia and asthma. I was just like him in that way and he used to pretend, too. He pretended I wasn't his daughter."

"Wait!" Deanna put her hand up. "Stop! What do you mean you weren't his daughter?"

"That was one of the things he whispered into my ear when he fondled my breasts," I uttered.

"And what else?" She would not be diverted, I could see that.

"He said my mother wasn't a virgin when they got married and so he wasn't sure I was his." I felt the old shame spread slowly through me and I shuddered. I remembered the mornings of my adolescence. Waking with my ever-present shame alive in my awareness and yet a small sane voice would ask, *How can you be guilty of anything? You haven't even gotten out of bed yet.* But my guilt was ever present. My guilt was the foundation of my life. "I want to ski through it," I said.

"Well, now that's obscure!" Kelly was back at me again.

I shrugged. "It's a northern thing. I need to face winter, Kelly. I need to face my father. Here. I wrote about my father and winter in my journal." I paged quickly to the entry.

He was a hunter. I remember him with a stag on the left fender. A stag with ten points. The slender drooping head. It always seemed to me that the neck was broken. I wasn't sure because the head with its huge liquid eyes and the slim muzzle lay on the metal curve of the fender at an odd angle. Or maybe it was where the bullet had entered. The delicate hoofed legs were stiff with death and Arctic cold.

My father was noted for his clean kills. He always put the bullet into the head or the neck and so at first I would think that the whole of the beast was there on the shining maroon fender of the DeSoto but then the emptiness would creep into my awareness. I knew that the fur was covering the gutting. There were no intestines, no heart, liver, or kidney. It was just meat inside there. Bones and muscles and venison. The antlers knobby and warm to the touch were taken away by my mother and she had them mounted for him in a velvet padding on a board of walnut. Polished antlers, ivory and forest brown. The hide was thrown away. The hooves tossed and the eyes gone forever.

The butcher made venison steaks, roasts and sausage. Venison pork sausage. Venison ground up and stuffed into pork guts. They were delicious. Rich and greasy, spicy and wild. They were sausages that oozed. Dripping chins. Bursting sausages wrapped in white home-made bread covered with mustard. Winter food brought home by my father at a great cost to us all.

Deer hunting season fell on their wedding anniversary every December and he'd go off to the woods and the snow with his elegant guns and his red hat with the ear flaps, his red wool jacket and trousers and long underwear. All this would be reverently unearthed from mothballs. He would flee to the north woods with his whiskey and his brothers. They wore red clothing to prevent shooting each other in the forest. He was so handsome with his black hair and his blue eyes.

If only he had taken me with him. I was so much like him in this. I ran away to the wild places as soon as I could get free. Always out to the woods, meadows, pastures. But he didn't take me. Only boys were allowed.

By Christmas time I would be wrapped in blankets sitting by a window watching the snow and the sleds and my brothers and sisters, older now, flinging themselves into snowbanks without me. I was sickly. Mother would rage about the house with her broom muttering about the cost of hunting. She regarded the northern winter as a personal insult and she held my father responsible for it. She has never forgiven him for taking her away from her California dream.

I shut the journal. "Maybe that's why I'm in California. And yet, I'm like my father. I'm still roaming around in the wilderness. I backpack and I hike and I know the mountains of the high Sierra. But now I want winter, too. I want to learn cross-country skiing. I'm going. I think it's important. Case closed," I added defiantly.

* * * * *

I flew to Seattle to meet Maggie and we drove together to the ski resort in Montana. Kathleen, DeeDee, and Stella were coming together from Nevada.

Fresh snow lay on the roadside, in the folds of the high mountains, on the branches of evergreens. Kathleen pronounced it the best powder of her extensive skiing career. The temperature was a crisp five degrees below zero but the sun shone brilliantly from a pure blue sky. It was winter with manners.

Maggie and I settled into the two-room suite on the ground floor of the resort. A sliding-glass door opened to the frozen lake beyond. I knew that after my first cross-country ski lesson I would step into my skis and stride right out the door down to the lake and stride mile after mile on the smooth surface, only the blue tips of my long, narrow skis visible beneath the fluffy cover of new powdered snow.

Maggie said, "I wonder how long it'll take them to get here. The weather reports weren't too good. They may have trouble on the road south of here." She poured kahlua into her hot chocolate and mine.

"What are we going to do about these beds?" I asked.

"Yeah, I've been thinking we need to ask the hotel for some rollaways so we can all sleep in one room,'" she replied.

That settled, I asked, "do you think we can get Stella and DeeDee to talk to each other this trip?"

"That was weird, wasn't it?" she answered. "I'm still not sure you should have forced them the way you did."

I wasn't sure either but after I had noticed on the houseboat that the two of them never spoke directly to each other and that DeeDee only spoke when Stella did, I bullied Kathleen and Maggie into leaving them in the galley together. We three oldest sisters went up top and waited under the stars.

Stella and DeeDee seemed to be hooked up to some peculiar switching mechanism. Stella would start; DeeDee would suddenly come to life and interrupt Stella. Stella would fall back into silence like a mechanical doll turned off. We waited and waited but there was no further sound below us in the night. No rise and fall of voices in rage or laughter. Nothing. We gave up and descended the ladder to find them sitting sullenly on either side of the tiny galley staring at the floor. "Well?" I asked.

"There's nothing to say," Stella answered.

The words had barely passed Stella's lips when DeeDee interjected, "I really resent this, Annie. There's nothing to talk about."

This was so obviously untrue that I had been flummoxed into inaction. But now, in Idaho, we were going to try to get something going between them.

And suddenly they were there. Doors flung open. Icy blasts of air whooshing down hallways. Luggage, skis, boots, brown grocery bags everywhere. Maggie and I marched back and forth from room to automobile as they breathlessly complained of icy roads, darkness, driving into snowbanks, being late, being here. When the unloading was completed, DeeDee waylaid me in the hallway. Stella grabbed me by the arm. I was pleased to be captured. They dragged me off to a public restroom. Kathleen was with Maggie in the suite.

Stella's cheeks were bright with cold and excitement. "Look!" she cried as she whipped a red wig out of a shopping bag. She waved the shopping bag at me. "We have four of them!"

DeeDee jumped in, "And I have the makeup!" She triumphantly banged a tube of pink gloss down on the bathroom counter. "And! And! Wait! Wait!" She was leaping about the mirrored room in a frenzy, digging through her purse. "Ah, here!" She slapped down eye shadow and a brush. "Blue! Just like Maggie's."

"Huh?" I said not too brightly.

This set the two of them laughing. Stella managed to get out, "And we made up a poem, too." She jammed the red wig over her brown short hair. I wondered if that was her real color. It looked good. "Here. Put yours on."

I was beginning to catch on. I pulled the wig down over my own frizzed hair. I painted my lips with Maggie's color and dusted my eyelids with her blue eye shadow. They did the same. "How much did the wigs cost?" I asked, thereby beginning the endless divvying of expenses which took place on all of our sister trips.

"Three ninety-nine each," answered Stella promptly, blotting her lipstick with a square of toilet paper.

"Memorize this!" DeeDee commanded.

I leaned over the counter and read aloud, "Maggie, Maggie, how she sings and dances through the night, smokes cigarettes and chews gum with great might."

"I have some gum right here," said Stella, handing me a stick. "Keep reading."

"Give her some Tab and great noises appear. Not only from the front, but also the rear." I muffled a giggle.

"Memorize!" DeeDee insisted. "Kathleen can keep her occupied only so long."

"She's a Leo and requires lots of attention along with other things we won't mention," I read obediently.

"I've got to pee," announced Stella.

"She looks at the scale and diets and diets. After a week of starvation, she causes a riot." I turned the page over. "How long is this anyway?"

"Not much longer. Do!" DeeDee pointed at the paper.

"With her sisters so dear and so near, she will surely give a great cheer. Maggie, Maggie, our red-headed sister, we truly can't resist her!"

I turned around and my two littlest sisters stood triumphantly before me with glowing faces under identical red wigs. I pulled them to the mirror with me and the three of us did look like Maggie. We crept down the hallway to our rooms, giggles escaping like air bubbles.

We knocked on the door and Kathleen answered. "Wait, wait!" She didn't laugh. She was very stern keeping her lips pressed tightly together.

"You promised!" She shouted back into the suite. "Eyes closed or into the snowbank and snow down your back and I'll have help!"

"I promise," said Maggie with false meekness.

Kathleen let us in, pushing us into the bathroom where Maggie couldn't see. She jammed the wig down over her head. It was crooked, blonde tendrils escaping in the back. DeeDee stuffed them in while Kathleen smeared gloss on her lips. "Hurry, hurry!" Stella urged. I jumped around mumbling, "Maggie, Maggie, our red-headed sister, we truly can't resist her." Kathleen had the eye shadow on now. Stella handed out unlit cigarettes. The smoking agreement was in force—no smoking in the suite itself. We got our gum working. "I have eye shadow on my nose," Kathleen complained. "Who cares?" said DeeDee and shoved her out the door.

"Does she know the poem?" Kathleen asked DeeDee grimly. All three looked at me doubtfully.

"You've had hours!" I protested.

"It will just have to do," DeeDee decided. With Kathleen threatening Maggie with further mayhem if her eyes weren't shut, we made our entrance. Maggie sat on the sofa with her eyes scrunched together, her shoulders tense with anticipation.

Kathleen raised her hand. We took a breath. She lowered it and together we shouted, "Now!"

She opened her eyes and I saw how truly blue they were. As blue as the sapphire set in a silver ring, which we gave her later. Before she could even finish her gasp, before the twitch of her lips gave way to guffaws and bellows, we were into the skit. I remembered about half of the poem but I made up for it by dancing around and waving my cigarette and cracking my gum on the words I didn't know. Maggie held herself as though she would explode. She rocked back and forth on the sofa.

We carried her off to dinner in the hotel lounge before she had a chance to protest being seen with us. We wore sweatshirts supplied by Stella announcing our Second Sister Reunion. As we walked to our table, DeeDee complained loudly, "Maggie, adjust your wig! Really!" We made the desired impact on the other restaurant patrons and ended up with two bottles of champagne and one bottle of a good California Chablis.

The next morning I went off with my ski instructor to a mountain meadow while the other four drove to the slopes. "You'll be all alone out there," Maggie protested.

"I'll be just fine," I insisted, knowing that Maggie ran in a group whenever she could.

My instructor was a six-foot-five giant who looked as though he had just been transported from Norway. He had a quiet patience which suited the perfect stillness of the snow-covered meadow with its etched track cut into the new snow. He taught me the diagonal stride that day and I knew I had conquered winter at last. There would be no more wistful peering into the forest from automobile windows for me. No more cabin fever. I had the run of the woods at last. I shed clothing along with burdens stuffing my down jacket into my fanny pack. I wore red knickers, blue wool knee-high stockings, a blue turtleneck, long-sleeved cotton shirt, a red wool hat and blue wool gloves. I glided step after step with a light covering of sweat starting up all over my skin, under my breasts, down my back. I had glided into the runner's high by my fourth mile and all I knew was exhilaration. Breathe, glide. Breathe, glide. Breathe, glide. "Keep that head up. It's a natural movement. Your feet know what to do." I raised my head and the sun sparkled on the snow. There were secrets on the other side of the mountain through the trees. I headed that way. "Wait!" he cried out. "Not that way. You don't know any turns yet. Tomorrow we'll practice step turns." I glided toward him and we skied back to the road.

When I got back to the hotel, I found the downhill skiers comparing notes. "We left our lesson after ten minutes," Kathleen announced.

"We hated the instructor," Maggie added. Her freckles had popped and her cheeks were pink.

I propped my skis in the closet and went back out into the hallway where Stella and DeeDee sat together on the floor resting their backs against the wall. An ashtray lay between them. They tapped their cigarettes into it from time to time. "How was your day?"

"Okay," said Stella glumly.

"Well, the instructor said right away that Kathleen and Maggie should have an intermediate lesson. I've never skied in high mountains before, you know." DeeDee lifted her chin in defiance, daring me to comment. When I shrugged she went on, "So I finished up my lesson and then I spent the day going up and down the slopes by myself. Tomorrow I go out with those two in there. I'm ready!" She pointed with her filtered cigarette and laughed anxiously. "And what happened to you anyway?" This question was directed at Stella. "I didn't see you at all after the lesson."

But Stella didn't answer. She got up from the floor heavily, pulling the strap of her heavy purse up over her shoulder. "I'm out of cigarettes."

"Aren't you going swimming with us?" I called after her as she marched away down the dark hallway.

"I'll meet you there later," she flung over her shoulder as she vanished.

"DeeDee, what's going on?"

"Got me," DeeDee said as she rose from her cross-legged position against the wall. "She showed up just in time to ride back to the hotel with us. Hasn't said more than ten words altogether to anybody since then." She brushed at a damp spot on her ski pants. "Sure is nice not to be pregnant for a change."

"You look good," I told her.

"I know," she said, and stuck her tongue out at me. We linked arms and burst into the suite. "Let's go swimming now that we have the Lone Ranger back."

The four of us changed into bathing suits, robes and slippers. We carried towels and we screamed when we had to walk in snow with only slippers on our bare feet. The pool was heated but open to the sky. The sun was setting and the sky was streaked with pinks and scarlets. The heated water created a fog. We flung ourselves gratefully into the hot water groaning and moaning with pleasure and then, incredibly, it began to snow. Large, individual flakes drifting lazily down through sunlight and fog. We lay on our backs floating. We stuck our tongues out to catch snowflakes.

"Best powder I've ever skied," Kathleen said smiling at the sky above her.

"Up to our thighs," added Maggie dreamily, paddling by.

"Tomorrow." said DeeDee.

"Step turns," I mumbled happily.

Stella was waiting for us in the suite when we got back. "I've already taken my shower," she pointed out defensively, and went out into the hallway for another smoke. We looked at each other but said nothing. We hoped that whatever it was would go away if we ignored it.

At dinner Maggie announced the solution to the bed problem. "If they won't give us any extra beds, I propose we steal them. I've spotted two rollaways in the hallway at the other edge of the lodge one floor up from us."

By ten that night all was quiet. Skiers tend to go to sleep early. We had donned our dark blue tee shirts given to us by Maggie. The seal announced that we were members of the Ladies Terrorist Society and Sewing Circle. Even Stella had pulled her tee shirt over her large breasts. She offered to scout the second floor, and she returned five minutes later puffing. "All's clear but I think we'll have to carry them one flight down because people are using the elevator."

"But that means through the kitchen!" Maggie pointed out.

"I've checked that out too. All dark. Not a soul around. Ready?" She looked happy.

"Ready," Maggie agreed and followed Stella down the hallway, gesturing for the rest of us to follow.

"Fucking bed is heavy," I muttered moments later as I struggled down the staircase. DeeDee was on the other end above me.

"Hurry up, you guys!" Maggie wheezed as she tried to stop herself from falling into DeeDee right behind her.

"Shush!" Stella hissed at the top of the stairs. "Somebody's coming!"

We froze. " How do I get myself into these things?" I asked DeeDee. But it was a false alarm and then we were on the ground floor and we raced in teams through the kitchen, the deserted dining room, and into the narrow darkened hallway. "Faster!" DeeDee spit at me. "They're gaining on us."

I looked back. It was true. Maggie's jaw was set and I could see that she was going to try to take us on the turn out of the dining room. "One of the wheels won't work!"

"I don't care," said DeeDee. "Pick it up and move your ass!" But while Maggie was swearing at Kathleen for pushing her into the door jamb, DeeDee and I shot through the other swinging door into the hallway. Stella had run ahead and opened the door to our suite and as we won the race by crossing the threshold first she complained that we made enough noise to wake the dead. But DeeDee leaned happily on the rollaway bed and announced, "Ha! Beat you two at something today!"

"It will never happen again," Kathleen promised as she closed the door behind her.

"You pushed me into the wall!" Maggie was outraged.

"Did not!"

"Did too!"

"You had a little help," I reminded DeeDee.

"Now what?" It was Stella, and her question punched a hole in our silliness.

Kathleen looked her in the eye. "Now we will set up this suite the way we like it." This meant having three beds in one room so that the five of us could talk in the dark. Otherwise we would spend a considerable part of the night saying, "What I can't hear you. What did she say? Would you say that again?"

"I might even get some sleep tonight instead of spending all my time going back and forth between rooms," Maggie sighed. She hated missing anything.

"Well, since I won the race. . . ." DeeDee hesitated and looked at me. "Since we won the race, I think Annie and me should get first dibs on what beds we want."

"What!" Kathleen and Maggie shouted simultaneously.

"And what about Stella!" I added virtuously. "She was a great scout."

110

And so we swept over Stella's gloom like an avalanche and rearranged the suite to our specifications. The room facing the lake was now a place to talk, eat, lay about and store clothing. Despite these arrangements I was beginning to wonder if all the action wasn't really taking place in the hallway. Now Maggie could be found filching cigarettes from both DeeDee and Stella and two ashtrays littered the carpeted floor. Kathleen and I frequently found ourselves alone in the suite looking at each other with raised eyebrows.

The next two days were more of the same. I headed out alone to the meadows with one car to meet my instructor and the other four took Kathleen's station wagon to the ski lifts. Stella disappeared the moment the other three sat down on the lift. She came out each day in ski gear No one saw her skiing. But she was always there when the afternoon sun was casting long shadows over the slopes. Her disappearances and silences were beginning to cast their own long shadows over our reunion.

On the fourth morning she announced that she wanted to ski with me. We all brightened at that and off we went together.

This time the instructor was a slim woman with long blonde braids. She took us up the slopes and taught us side stepping and the snow plow and we practiced step turns. Because Stella was an alpine skier, she was able to execute the turns with more skill than I could muster even though she had never before put on the long, skinny cross-country ski which is attached to the ski boot only by the toe. We puttered away a good part of the morning and then we went out on the trail. Stella fell far behind and as I waited for her to catch up, I realized that cross-country skiing was the worst thing she could have chosen for herself. The aerobic demand was far beyond her physical condition. I examined her clinically as she huffed her way up the trail and then stopped for a cigarette.

"She has chosen the slow death," I decided aloud. Smoking and drugs and booze.

The instructor glided over to me as I looked back down the trail at my small sister smoking under an evergreen tree in the frosty air. I shivered. The instructor followed my gaze. She said, "I would teach you more but your sister is not very strong and so it slows things down."

My resentment was stimulated and at the end of the day I said, "Stella, I want to go out by myself tomorrow. You already know more about skiing than I do and I want to learn as much as I can in the short time I have here. This is my first time." My shoulders hunched up, bracing for the storm.

"I'm too slow for you, aren't I?" she said bitterly.

"Yes."

"Not good enough for you! Well, forget it. Just forget it!" She slammed the car door and punished me by smoking cigarettes in the car all the way back to the lodge. I opened my window to the icy fresh air and wondered how long the guilt would last. I noticed, however, that under my guilt was something else. Anger.

Stella had taken control of the reunion. All pretense at her participation in the ski vacation had been abandoned. The tension grew hour by hour. We didn't know what to do.

On the last day Stella did not leave the lodge at all. After skiing, the four of us gathered in the suite. Stella was gone. We roamed restlessly in the small space like herd animals before a thunderstorm.

I found Maggie in the bathroom. I rubbed hand cream into my chapped fingers while Maggie leaned over the counter and looked at herself in the mirror. She pushed her hair around aimlessly. "Where is she? It's our last night. We're supposed to have this nice dinner together." She repeated her question to DeeDee and Kathleen who were playing cards in the other room. They had no answer. "Well," said Maggie impatiently, "I've had it. I'm going to go and find her!"

I dried my hair and paced. I looked at the brown rugs and the dull light and the long windows opening to the lake. Fog had moved in and all the subtle shades of white were there. White fog moving slowly east, the powdered snow ankle deep on the thick ice beneath, the ice with a faint touch of blue in it. Trees were shrouded in snow and fog, they loomed all along the edges of the lake which stretched for miles beyond my vision. I had spent an unhappy day skiing without Stella. Kathleen and DeeDee were now playing cards, without talking.

Maggie raged in with a piece of paper in her hand.

"Well, did you find her?" Kathleen inquired mildly. I was learning that as things got crazier, Kathleen got calmer. DeeDee held a card in mid-air, waiting for Maggie's answer.

Maggie waved the hotel stationery at us. "Oh, I found her. In the bar, where else? She gave me this."

As Maggie stood there fuddled with the folded letter in her hand, I noticed a note in the litter on one of the tables. There was a photograph with the note.

Stella had scrawled, "I took a picture of myself in the mirror but there was no one there." And she was right. The photograph revealed only a flash of light and a glimpse of the side of a curved hand.

"Look!" I thrust the note and the photograph at them. DeeDee took it first and shuddered, handing it to Kathleen who handed it to Maggie who read it and dropped it impatiently back into the trash on the table top. "What am I supposed to do with this?" She took the letter.

"Read it!" pronounced DeeDee.

"What did she tell you?"

Maggie turned to Kathleen. "That she'd be done in a little while. Ah, hell, I've had it." She opened the letter, smoothing it out on the card table. We leaned over it.

"You have all invaded my privacy and you will never, ever understand me anyway because I'm not here."

"What does this mean?" Maggie's voice was small, hurt, bewildered. We fluttered about the rooms reeling and pacing and gathering anger as we moved.

She appeared in our midst quietly.

"Have you been drinking?" I wanted to know.

"No," she replied with a little smile.

She didn't smell drunk but it was hard to tell. We were all bunched up at the door facing her. "Why are you doing this? What does this letter mean?" Maggie waved it at her.

She came into the suite and we backed up to let her in. She closed the door behind her. "You just don't understand anything, do you?" She went to the inner room with its windows on the lake. She bent down to a brown grocery bag in her corner of the room and rummaged about muttering, "I can't find my cigarette lighter." She tossed underwear, combs, pens, shoes, hairbrushes.

"Don't you have a suitcase?" Maggie inquired irritably and I realized that I had been watching Stella engage in a continual sorting process for the past four days. Her five brown paper grocery bags were limp and mushy from her constant handling, and as I saw her there on her knees, I understood that the only difference between my sister and those women on the street with their little red wagons or shopping carts and piles of bags was that they were on the street and my sister was still inside.

"Have any of you seen my lighter?" she was shrieking and DeeDee handed her a book of matches. She declared war by lighting up and sitting down in an overstuffed chair. No hallway, not even an open window. She blew smoke into the room. We followed DeeDee into the inner room. Kathleen moved behind the table as though she needed a barrier between her and Stella.

DeeDee put her hands on her hips and, for the first time, she addressed Stella directly. "I really resent this. We came here for a good time."

Stella looked up at DeeDee towering over her. She blew smoke through her nostrils and said, "So what?" The skin around her eyes was pulled back as though the intensity of her rage had consumed the softness of her round cheeks and hollowed them. Her eyes were brutal. Eyes as weapons. If looks could kill.

"You're drunk! And just like all drunks, there's always an excuse. You do it because you're drinking or you're drinking because things are so tough. I'm not going to put up with this." DeeDee moved away from Stella and stomped around the room.

"I haven't been drinking!"

"Then why are you behaving this way? Why don't you get help like Annie?"

She leaned back in her chair and took another drag. "Well, excuse me!" she drawled sarcastically.

"I'm sick of this. You and the bottle and the bottle and you!"

At that Stella sprang out of the chair, dropping the cigarette butt on the floor where it smoldered in the carpet. She crossed the room in three gallops and slapped DeeDee across the face.

DeeDee grabbed her by both shoulders and screamed over and over, "I am not responsible for your childhood. I'm not. It's not me!"

Kathleen plucked the butt from the burning carpet. Maggie and I reached them both at the same time. Stella's head rocked back and forth from DeeDee's shaking grip. I put my hands on Stella's arms just as she was tensing for another attack. Her hands were twisted into claws with the dried blood nails flashing. Her face was twisting and contorting. Maggie now had DeeDee by the shoulders and she pulled her away from Stella. "That will be enough of that," she ordered.

A phrase from the Battered Women's Shelter policy manual popped in my head and I quoted it, "Violence is not

115

acceptable. It's okay to be angry but violence is not acceptable."

Kathleen was frozen back at the table. I hoped that she would start breathing soon and stop looking like a statue. DeeDee went to the table and lit her own cigarette. Stella sat down on the sofa on the opposite side of the room. Maggie hovered near DeeDee. I pulled the drapes shut. The sun had gone down. We were closed in by darkness.

Head down, DeeDee said softly, "Stella, I looked at pictures of us when we were kids and do you know what?" Stella glowered at her like a caged animal. "When I was twelve, I was five feet, four inches tall and you were a skinny little kid who didn't come up to my chest. Why do you think I wanted to hang out with Kathleen instead of you?"

Oh! I thought. Oh.

"Cow!" Stella screamed it at her. It was the old name-calling.

DeeDee winced. She had had an awkward adolescence and Kathleen was one of those girls who had passed from the 4th of July Parade Queen at three to Homecoming Queen at seventeen without a pimple or a loose strand of hair.

"We love you, Stella." It was Kathleen with her quiet voice. "Why do you fight us?"

But Stella was on her knees again searching through her bags. "My lighter, where's my lighter?"

I couldn't stand it. "Get help, Stella, get help!"

She reared up in fury. "I hate you. I hate you all. Get out of this room! All of you!" She was hopping with rage. Her heavy breasts bounced under the ski sweater.

We crept away and lay in the dark in separate rooms. We packed glumly the next morning. Kathleen retreated into a contemplative funk. "This wasn't good. It shouldn't have happened."

Maggie tried to fix it. She stopped DeeDee and Stella in the hallway on one of the many trips to the automobiles. With

116

a cheery tone she said, "Now you two make up and try to feel good about each other." She fussed around them trapping them in the narrow passage. "You both got your feelings hurt but you really love each other and you should remember that." They simultaneously walked away from her in opposite directions leaving her mumbling in futility to the walls.

When Stella walked by me I stopped her. "I will never allow you to blackmail me this way again."

She removed my hand from her shoulder with one of her long pointed nails and moved away without speaking.

She maintained her iced rage, her furious silence for the entire twelve hours it took Kathleen and DeeDee to drive them all back to Boulder City.

8

"Maggie's coming to Los Angeles just to visit me," I announced proudly to the group. "And she's oming to a counseling session with me too."

Deanna gave one of those smiles of fond indulgence. "Annie, I think you should tell the group what happened on your skiing trip with your sisters. Particularly what happened when Stella, Kathleen and DeeDee got back to Boulder City."

"Hey, you're getting all the names straight now. That's pretty good. There are so many of us." But while I babbled I felt a wave of sadness wash through me.

When they got back to Boulder City, Kathleen and Stella dropped DeeDee off at Mother's apartment where she was to spend the night before flying back to Wisconsin. DeeDee, who was still devastated by Stella's behavior, confided it all to Mother. DeeDee also explained that she had been doing research on alcoholism and was convinced that Stella was an alcoholic and we were all enablers. That we helped Stella be an alcoholic and this included Mother as well.

Lily excused herself at the end of this impassioned explanation and said she had to go to the grocery store to pick up a few things. "I'll be right back!" she called out as she closed the front door.

But Lily didn't go to the supermarket. Instead she drove to Stella's house and repeated everything DeeDee had just communicated and, while Lily was in transit again between her two youngest daughters, Stella broke her silence. And this time it was not the childhood names of "pig" and "cow." This was the vile mouth of a whore. Stella shrilled into the telephone, "Cunt! Cocksucker! Twat! I'll kill you. I hate you. You keep your fucking cunt face shut about me. You pig-faced, fat cunt!" There was more but DeeDee quietly hung up and unplugged the phone so that she would not have to listen to it ring. Then she made up the sofabed, turned out all the lights, and pretended to be sleeping when Lily came back.

Elaine looked me straight in the eye, "What do you want from your Mother, Annie?"

"Leave me alone!"

"I think she needs to write another Mother Letter." Elaine's plump face was strained and tired. "How do you feel about what your Mother did?"

"Did?"

"Yeah, did. To your two sisters. I think it's pretty rotten, don't you?"

"I guess so," I said doubtfully.

"What's going on, Annie?" Deanna with one of her timely, pertinent interrogatories.

"I feel as though I'm looking at this from the wrong end of a telescope where everything is so small and so far away that I can't feel much about it at all." I scratched my head and glanced quickly at Kelly who had said that her hair was falling out from the stress of this incest therapy.

"I have a new bald patch right here," she had confirmed. "The doctors say it will grow back."

I continued, "It seems I hear a voice that says why bother, what's the fuss. Stuff like that."

Elaine asked, "And whose voice do you think it is?"

I said the three forbidden words. "I don't know."

Deanna groaned. "Annie, write another Mother Letter for next week."

"But Maggie's coming and I want to be ready for her. Don't you think I should write a letter to her or something?"

"Do you?"

"Yes," I said defensively.

"The week after, then." Elaine demanded.

"The week after," I agreed.

But when Maggie showed up, I hadn't written anything at all. I was too busy doing housework. I wanted to prove to her that I wasn't a slob. I cleaned cupboards. I scrubbed floors. I rearranged the closets. I vacuumed. I dusted. I even washed windows on the outside. "A great place, Annie," she said as I took her on the tour. "Did Laura ever live here with you?"

"No, why do you ask?"

"Oh, I just wonder about her. Do you hear from her?"

"No, no I don't." There was an old pain like a hand pressing down on my sternum.

"Anybody else in your life?" She hung a violet wool dress on a padded hanger in my closet.

"Not now."

She faced me with her intense blue eyes. "I never told you this but I was glad you had Laura and I was sorry when it ended."

120

"Thanks, Maggie." I gulped. "Do you have any laundry? I even have my own washer and dryer. No more laundromats." But she said she didn't. I retreated to the bathroom and shut the door. I wasn't quite sure what was wrong but I knew I was afraid; my heart was jumping in my chest and my hands were wet.

"Shouldn't we go?" she called out. "It's almost three. How long does it take to get there?"

"I'm coming." I was calmer by the time we got to the Pacific Therapy Center. Deanna was waiting in her white-on-white office with the glass tables and wastebaskets. "This is Maggie," I said comparing Deanna's strawberry coif to Maggie's vibrant red curls. I was white-on-white myself next to these two.

Maggie and I sat down together on a couch facing Deanna, who was on one of her inevitable thrones; this one a white overstuffed easy chair. Maggie and I looked at her expectantly. "Well, Annie, why don't you start?"

"Start? Start what?" I said wildly, looking around the room.

"Don't you have something to say to Maggie?"

I looked at Maggie. She was so kindly. I remembered that I always thought of her as Greatheart even when we were estranged for almost ten years. "Yeah, whatever happened to that?"

"To what?" Maggie responded patiently.

"Remember when I came back from California the first time and I told you about losing my virginity and then you decided I was a moral criminal and you didn't want to be seen with me in public?"

And she laughed. "Oh my God. Ain't it the truth? How times have changed. How I've changed." Her eyes clouded. "I think it was Mother. She was always setting us up to not like each other. Remember how she called you smart and me dumb?"

"Yeah." We were facing each other on the couch. Our breathing was synchronized.

"Do you forgive me?" she asked.

"I did long ago," I said, understanding suddenly that I had. "Long ago."

"Me too." We breathed some more and then we were done with that. There was a long pause.

"Maggie," said Deanna softly, "Annie's been working very hard here and what she had to do to survive in your family was miraculous. How did you survive it?"

"I'm not sure what you mean."

Deanna continued her gentle prodding. "You two may be from the same family but you each had your own experience. Annie was the oldest and so she had enormous responsibilities."

"Responsibilities?" She echoed this doubtfully.

"Yes," I interjected. "I never played after school, remember? I had to go straight home and help Mother with the little ones and if I didn't I felt so guilty."

"Ummm, yes. I never thought about it before. It's true." She examined me as though she had never quite seen me before.

"So how did you survive, Maggie?" Deanna asked her again.

"I made friends. I stayed out of the house. I was always in a group of my pals. I went to their house. I didn't have any jobs after school until Annie left home and then I got Mother."

"Right." I added, "And when *you* left home, Kathleen got Mother."

"I suppose we passed her down from one sister to the next like a, like a. . . ." She faltered.

"Burden," I put in, finishing her sentence.

She shifted uneasily. "This is all in the past. Can't we just forget it and love each other?"

122

"Maggie, I'm not going to let you wallpaper this over with one of your Hallmark card sentiments." I was shaking. How dare I be angry with Maggie?

Deanna ignored me. She addressed Maggie. "That was a good way you picked to survive in your family, wasn't it?"

Now her eyes were filled with tears brimming and quaking above her lower lashes. "I thought it worked pretty well."

Now it was my turn to see Maggie as I had never seen her before. "We're different people, aren't we? And it's okay, isn't it?"

"It's better than okay, Annie," Deanna said. "It's the way it's supposed to be. Why don't you two go and spend the day together getting acquainted? Play!" she commanded. As we moved to the door she stopped me, "Tell Maggie about the Teddy Bear incident."

"Teddy Bear?" asked Maggie as I fastened my seat belt.

"It's embarrassing. Do you want to drive up the coast and have an early dinner? "I'll tell you then."

When we pulled into the restaurant parking lot she prodded, "Teddy Bear?"

"Okay! Okay! We were given an assignment to spend time playing."

"Your incest therapy group?"

"Right, and we were supposed to buy ourselves a toy and be really nice to ourselves and have fun."

"So, what happened?"

"Well, everybody in the group had a marvelous time. Buying rubber duckies and playing in the bathtub and reading what they had written about it to the rest of us."

I squirmed. "Let's go into the restaurant."

"Come on, tell!"

I locked the car and we walked toward the Sea Lion Restaurant, a place of barely edible seafood but with tables hanging out over the ocean and waves smashing on the glass walls. "I thought I was being so clever. I waited until the night

123

was almost over. I was hoping they'd forget me altogether, but no such luck. It was my turn and so I read what I'd written which was that I would like to get over my hard-hearted attitude about teddy bears."

"You don't like teddy bears?" She stopped walking and thought this over. "You never were a child, were you?"

"No, not really. I didn't have time."

We walked to the restaurant glumly, arm in arm. The waitress took us to one of the tables on the ocean and we watched the ceaseless waves. I said, "I wasn't really a teenager either. I always admired you for yelling at Mother when you were in high school."

"You did? You admired me?"

"I didn't dare yell at her and I think that's the time when you're supposed to separate from your mother and father. The time to rebel and become a separate person but I didn't dare. I wanted to, though."

"Well, why didn't you?" She frowned at the red snapper floating in cooking oils on her plate.

"I thought she'd send me away again. Throw me out of the family like she did when I was fourteen." I pushed limp green beans around with a bent fork.

"But we were all so jealous of you for getting away and the hell out of there!"

"I know, but think of it from my point of view. My own mother didn't want me in the family—and now I think the only reason she let me come back is because father was gone by then, living in Milwaukee."

Maggie smashed her red snapper into her mashed potatoes.

"I tore up all the pictures I had of Mother and me together."

"What?"

"I tore them up before the ski trip. I couldn't stand it. It's such a lie." I watched her closely. Would she reject me now?

124

She pushed her plate away and sipped ice water. "You tore up all the pictures. You're really angry with her, aren't you?"

"Yes."

"This makes me so uncomfortable but I think I see your reasons." She sighed. "Aren't you a little obsessed with all this? I mean, can't we just get this behind us?"

"I'd like to do that but I'm not done yet, and Maggie, you will probably need therapy too."

"Why? I was never molested."

"Yeah, but you were there when it was going on."

"I can't stand this. I don't want to talk about it any more. Okay? Let's get out of here."

"Okay. Do you want to walk on the beach?"

"Yes, but let's take off our shoes and socks."

* * * * *

It was my thirty-fifth Tuesday night and I reported that my sister, Maggie, did love me because she hadn't rejected me even when I told the truth about how I felt about our mother. I had somehow slid by the assignment to write another Mother letter and fallen into the group assignment which was to write a letter to the Real Self.

Dear Real Self,

Thank you for being there. I am sorry that I haven't been paying attention to you when I should be. I have so many lapses.

My vanity, for example. My unreal self who rises up and says: "I'm the best. Nobody suffers as much as I do or as I have. I'm the best victim in the world. Nobody will ever understand me because what I have experienced is beyond what other people could handle

125

and so nobody, and I mean nobody, has the depth that I do.

So there. Take that! All you slipshod, moral misfits. You insensitive nobodies.

And about this love stuff? What a crock! You're all just making it up. Being happy and liking each other. Trusting and all that. I don't believe it for a minute. I am better than all of you and I can do without love, and besides—there is not enough love in the whole world to make up for what happened to me. So you can just take your love and shove it!"

The truth is, my Real Self knows I'm afraid of love and that I'm angry with anyone who raises love as a possibility. How scary that love might be real. That I might get some and be part of it. That I might have to surrender my victimhood.

Annie

I cried after I read that one and so did Melanie, of course. Susana didn't hand the tissue directly to Melanie. She took a few for herself and Kelly let loose with a teardrop or two.

I saw Maggie's face before me. It was filled with concern, with love. I could only peek at this face surreptitiously. It was almost more than I could bear.

Elaine nagged, "This is all very touching but where is this mother letter Annie keeps promising to write?"

"Deanna," I complained, "why is she after me like this?"

"She has her reasons," Deanna confided mysteriously.

"Are you ever going to get the goddam mother letter right?" Elaine yelled at me.

I yelled right back. "I'll write the goddam letter. Okay?"

"Okay!"

We glared at each other and panted for breath. The following showed up the very next Tuesday night.

Mother,

If you were dead, I would be free because then I wouldn't have to worry so much about telling the truth about you, me, and the incest.

I wouldn't have to worry about you rejecting me and your power to get my sisters and brothers to reject me because I hurt Mother, the saint and martyr that we have all come to know and love.

If you were dead, I could breathe easy. I used to think my asthma came from Dad and his molestation but I now see you did it to me too by leaning on me. By crushing me to death with your needs, your confidences, your loneliness, your sexuality. You sucked my young energy heedlessly without thinking about me at all.

I want you to die so that I can live. It seems you tried to take my life so that you could live. It seems if I have my life for myself that I'm taking something from you. You trained me to think I have no right to live for myself. The right to just be. So I have been rescuing everybody and hating them for it at the same time. It's just like you. I deprive myself and then I hate everybody for that too.

I am in a death struggle with anyone who gets close to me. I think they are trying to kill me or take me over just like you did and to prevent that I become like you and take them over instead. I want to quell their desires, their personality and uniqueness so that I'll be safe. I gave up my own daughter because of this. I don't want to be either the killer or the killed.

When you asked, "Why didn't you bring your daughter to me?" I was astounded. No daughter of mine would ever be turned over to a killer like you or to a killer like me. See, I am different from you. I don't use my children to meet my own needs.

I want to be free of the ice around me. The numb-
ness and dumbness.

Annie

When I finished reading this I couldn't hear anything but a
roaring in my ears. I heard Deanna calling me from far away,
as though she were on the other side of a field and we were in
a tornado in prairie country. She came to me and lifted me up.
Kelly and Susana cleared away Deanna's chair and the stuffed
turtles on the floor. Elaine supported me on one side and
Deanna held me up on the other. They brought me to the new
space at the end of the room. I was hobbled and hunched.
Deanna put a red bataca in my hand. There was a chair in
front of me. Deanna asked, "Aren't you pissed off?"

I turned toward her slowly, in a great puzzlement. I was
sixty-five years old at that moment. My joints were stiff and
swollen with arthritis just like my Mother's. But Deanna was
not fooled by this. "Say: How dare you do that to me?"

The roaring got louder and I turned back toward the
chair. Somebody's arms raised the bataca high above my head.
I guess they were my arms and as the bataca came down onto
the seat of the chair everybody in the room disappeared. I was
in a tunnel at the small end, in the eye of the hurricane. I
wasn't much there either. What was there was rage. Pure rage.
Elemental, like a force of nature suddenly released. The room
was weirdly elongated and then it was just me. Me and the
rage. I don't remember speaking. I don't remember hitting.
They tell me that I did both for a long, long time. I know it
happened though, because the next day I couldn't move. The
muscles in my middle back ached, my arms ached and could
not be touched.

"That was hard work, Annie. It was equivalent to
chopping a cord of firewood. You don't usually use those
muscles." Deanna explained this to me by telephone the next
morning.

128

I dragged through the week sleeping ten and twelve hours each night. I felt drained of everything. Something huge was gone. Something I had had inside of me forever. I had been assigned no letter for the next week. I was to rest and just be.

But they didn't leave me drifting for long. Deanna said, "Annie, I want you to do another Mother Letter."

"What?"

"You heard me."

"But, but...." It was useless. Nag. Nag. Nag.

Dear Mother,

I am tired of worshipping at your altar. Of protecting you and your precious feelings and of stuffing my own feelings down to the point of wanting to do violence to you. I am choking on my rage toward you.

With you, it is always one thing or another. When I was little, you were always pregnant and hopeless. How dare I feel young and downtrodden? Lonely and without anyone? When father molested me, you got cancer. Upstaged again. Your tragedies were always more important than mine.

And then there's all those novenas to the Blessed Virgin Mary and all those letters to me about how you are praying for me. How could I possibly yell at a martyr like you? And now you are old and arthritic, having gallantly born and raised seven children. So how could I possibly be upset with you now? What right do I have to have all this hurt, humiliation, love and fury mixed up together?

Talking to you consists of two things. It's either mindless chitchat or your sex life. I am sick and tired of hearing about your sex life and which men can do it and which ones can't. And how you can't find the right one.

I can get more compliments from perfect strangers than I can from you. I can walk into your house after not seeing you for more than two years, looking really great and not one word from you. Not one. I don't know why this hurts so much but it does. You never told me that I was pretty, that you were proud of me. When I'm around you I usually feel ugly which is why I don't like being around you.

As to your mindless chitchat, I think that makes me crazier than anything else. All this stuff going on between you and me, and you demonstrate a total commitment to trivia. It doesn't matter that I'm over here suffering or feeling ugly or wanting to throttle you or to cry or laugh or even love you. I'm tired of you pushing me away when I tell you that I love you. I'm insulted when you tell me not to hug you because it hurts. I feel bitter and weary when you announce that I hate you.

Sometimes, I do hate you. I hate you for not protecting me from him. I hate you for not protecting me from you.

I love you too, as much as I don't want to admit it. I seem to be stuck with my love like my nose on my face.

Annie

The whole group, including Deanna, chorused simultaneously, "And what do you want from your Mother, Annie?"

This time I knew. "Two things. One you know. Stop talking to me about her sex life. The second one is that I want her to acknowledge my existence."

The moment I said it, I knew that I was truly ready to go see Lily. To break the silence I had maintained for months, all through the Christmas holidays. "My sisters are going to

130

Boulder City for Mother's Day. I think I'll go too. It's just a few weeks away."

I looked around the room. There were no dissenting votes. I had, for the first time in my life, support and approval for a personal decision. I looked my crystal turtle in the eye and I think he winked at me.

* * * * *

The California spring was coming and the sunlight flooded my bedroom window. I pulled on my nylon running shorts and my cotton tank top. I tied a blue bandana around my forehead as a sweat band. I stretched and bent and tied my shoelaces. I put my foot down on the graveled path and I knew that I was alone on the trail. At this early hour I had the forest to myself.

The trail wound narrowly through a strand of saplings and chaparral and the new spring leaves were covered with dew and raindrops from the night's rainfall. By the time I entered this gauntlet I was already wet with my own sweat and the sweet cold shower of water falling off leaves was a welcome pleasure. But then I became aware of the pain in my chest and I knew it was the grass I was smoking every night after work.

I stopped abruptly on the trail. The rain-soaked chaparral was giving up its spicy perfume to the morning sunlight. Why was I smoking dope every night anyway? I had been telling myself it was because I was having so much trouble at the dentist with all the root canal surgery and I couldn't take codeine because it made me throw up.

The sunshine had crept over to me as I stood in the path, shivering and thinking. I moved into it blindly, absently. And what about that one glass of wine at lunch that knocked me out for almost two hours in the middle of the day? And my pride that it was only one glass?

The sun was all around me now. Mist rose in lazy tendrils, drifting upward to a clean blue sky. "I'm doing it because I'm

131

afraid!" I shouted to the forest. "But I'm not afraid any more. I don't have anything to hide!"

I raised my arms to the sun. I pulled my wet tank top off over my head and stuffed it into the elastic band on my shorts and I ran bare-breasted in the morning toward the mountain. I danced on a flat, white rock above the tree tops while my shirt dried in the sun.

I was late to the office but I didn't care. That night I threw out all my wine and all my dope. I slept the sleep of angels.

I was late to group too but when I got there nobody scowled at me because Deanna was engrossed with Elaine. When Deanna got up and sat down next to her, I knew it was going to be scary. Deanna stroked Elaine's cheek. "We need to hear and you need to tell."

Elaine opened her mouth and a croak came out. She swallowed and tried again. "I drove to my parents' house on Sunday and I confronted them."

She sat solidly on the couch like some ancient image of the earth mother, heavy and full-breasted, full-bellied. I was riveted. My rosy fantasies of confrontation were now at risk.

"My husband came with me and I told them everything. Everything about Dad and my brothers and. . . ."

I interrupted her, "Your mother too? She was there? And all about what she did to you? The enemas?"

"Yes."

"What happened?" Kelly was squirming with impatience. Even Marsha sat up straight. Melanie prepared to weep. Christina repaired her lipstick and Susana readied herself with tissue boxes.

"They denied everything, of course. I expected that." She put both her feet flat on the floor. Deanna had moved back to her usual chair.

"How do you feel?" Melanie asked with trembling lower lip.

132

"Good. Okay." She seemed calm and steady but then she looked down at her folded hands.

"Tell them, Elaine." Deanna stared at her calmly.

"My mother had a stroke last Sunday night and my father and my brothers all called me separately and told me it was just as they had always predicted." She stopped.

"Which is?" Kelly asked greedily.

"That I would be the death of her and now I had done it!" Elaine twisted her hands together.

"Your three rapists called you up and told you that?" Marsha asked in her dead voice.

We all jumped, since we were so unused to Marsha saying anything. Elaine nodded sadly. I drifted away into a realization that my mother Lily was capable of such a thing. Dying so that she would not have to face the truth.

When I came back I heard Elaine saying, "I'm not allowed to go to the funeral."

I whispered to Melanie, "Is she dead?"

She jammed me in the ribs with her elbow. Most unlike the girlish Melanie, she hissed, "No, you fool! She's not expected to get through the night. Listen!"

"But I did manage to visit her at the hospital even though they tried to stop me. I called the doctor and I've made arrangements to go when the rest aren't there. Last night, we talked. Really talked to each other. We've made our peace." She smiled. It was a radiant smile filled with infinite sadness.

I stared at Elaine open-mouthed, slack-jawed. Deanna caught on to me. "What?"

"My mother, Lily, I'm trying to call her Lily, she could do this. She could die just to get out of it all." I did not take my eyes off Elaine's face. "I'm ready to see her now, Elaine." I went to Elaine and knelt down before her and she bent to embrace me and as our arms went around each other we mingled our bitter, salted tears.

* * * * *

I was ready. I had my hotel reservations. I had my car. I had my new clothes. I had a new hairstyle. I had contact lenses. I had my two conditions for a relationship with Lily. I had Elaine's example of courage. I had sobriety.

The impromptu sister reunion was DeeDee's impulse. She was on a mission to gain approval from Lily. She centered this longing around her own children, offering them up to Lily for a blessing which could never be obtained. This particular child was the little girl in DeeDee's womb on the houseboat trip. Kathleen's and my Goddess Daughter. It would be our introduction to her. Pearl was almost two-and-one-half years old now.

She clung to DeeDee's skirts, overwhelmed by the sudden attention and the shocking revelation that her mother was somehow profoundly attached to these large creatures called aunts. She stared at me resentfully, peeping out from behind DeeDee's thighs, torn between curiosity and shyness. She was the color of autumn leaves with her auburn hair and dark eyes. Her complexion was creamy white. She had looked over Stella's little boy, Jersey, and sized him up as no problem. She had an older brother after all and she knew how to handle him. She was also the daughter of a feminist and so even though Jersey was older by a year and more than two inches taller, she was stocky and square-shouldered and possessed of a fierce resolve. She knocked him to the ground with one great shove and asserted her authority. That settled, the two of them played joyfully, running everywhere.

I found myself chasing them down the suburban streets of Kathleen's neighborhood, terrified by the passing automobiles and my utter inability to catch either little hellion. But Pearl looked back and sensed that she had gone too far. She reined Jersey in and they trotted back to me laughing. Pearl had not yet acknowledged me nor called me by name. I waited.

I found her in the hallway at Kathleen's house later that afternoon. Alone, she was leisurely bouncing herself against the wall. Gently, with my back to the wall, I bounced too. A gleam of interest shot out of her eyes but flicked away when I tried to catch it. I turned my head away and kept bouncing, keeping time with her. We did not speak. My peripheral vision caught a smile and we moved a little closer to each other. We were in perfect rhythm now. I felt tall and she felt small but the nubby plaster wall joined us. As we thumped along pleasantly, DeeDee spotted us and galloped back to a bedroom where she scooped up a camera and tried to capture the two of us in that moment. But as soon as the camera came up to DeeDee's eye, Pearl scowled and stopped bouncing. DeeDee laughed. "She doesn't like to have her picture taken." I glanced down at Pearl and she shrugged her tiny shoulders and ran away.

We gathered in one of those Las Vegas restaurants designed for serious drinking and indifferent eating, unless prime rib and steak are important aspects of your diet. It was Stella's suggestion because she was coming directly from her shift at the Green Lounge. As we slid into the vinyl-padded booth, we chatted idly, trying to paste pleasantries over our tension. It would be the first time we had all been together since Stella's psychotic break in Idaho. As usual, we had a plan.

DeeDee and Stella had talked by telephone and all DeeDee would say was, "It's handled. Don't worry about it."

Maggie announced to Stella, "We want you to get therapy, Stella."

And Stella replied, "I don't have the money. I don't have the time. I can't find a therapist."

DeeDee looked around the table. "But we're rich, Stella."

Kathleen, Maggie and I examined each other in surprise. DeeDee was right. I didn't have to count potatoes at supper time anymore to be certain that everyone would get enough to eat. My business had expanded along with the new computer mania. DeeDee, Kathleen, and Maggie all had successful husbands and affluent suburban lives.

"Therefore," DeeDee added, "we are going to give you some money for therapy right now." Maggie handed her a check.

Stella protested but Maggie silenced her. "And don't worry about paying it back either. I also have a list of three of the most highly recommended therapists in this area." She handed her the neatly printed list of names, telephone numbers, addresses.

"Call us, Stella," I begged handing her my telephone credit card number. All our numbers were on Maggie's list.

She took these gifts silently, neither accepting nor rejecting them but simply going along with the program, as she would say.

In the ensuing lull I piped up. "What's different about me?"

They examined me carefully. "You *are* different somehow," DeeDee mused, leaning on her elbow. Maggie mumbled that I seemed more relaxed. I nodded. I also pointed out that I was more fun too but it was Kathleen who figured it out. "You're not wearing glasses!"

I smiled smugly. I was not more than five miles from Lily and in the same town and I didn't feel ugly.

And then Stella said, "Did you stop drinking too?" She pointed at my mineral water with one of her long red fingernails.

"That too. I just can't handle it."

"Umph!" said Maggie, putting her vodka tonic down on the table.

When we got to my hotel room, Stella dashed to the bathroom. We heard her gagging. She came out in a fury. "That scampi was contaminated. I just know it!" She called the restaurant and complained and we waited patiently. We had all been through it before. Stella shouting at the world.

136

The department store where Jersey had fallen. The disputes with her next-door neighbor over watering the lawn. Quarrels with her boss, her doctor, her dentists, her parade of roommates.

When she had finished, we pushed the bed back against the wall and we pulled the chairs around in a circle. The room was dark and it had the functional hotel decor. Brown rugs, chocolate brown drapes, brown and beige bedspread. I explained how the incest therapy group process worked. The overhead lamp threw a pool of light into our circle. We were in a womb of darkness with the light at the center.

I started with initiation. The old story. My story. "The incest began when I was twelve or earlier. I'm not sure when, but it doesn't matter anymore now that I'm willing to face it all. Anyway, Dad would take me into the living room after dinner and make me lie beside him on the couch. He would fondle my breasts while he watched television. Everybody else also watched television while this was going on, including Mother. It stopped when she sent me away to St. Francis School for Girls when I was fourteen. I never really lived with him again."

I paused. What I wanted to say wasn't really part of my story but it was a persistent, nagging thought and I wanted them to hear it. "I think Bri was trained to be what he is by watching Dad molest me. You were all there in the living room while it was going on. . . ." I trailed off, and when I raised my eyes I could see nods of agreement.

Encouraged I stood in front of each sister and asked, "Now that you've heard my story, what do you think of me?" My heart leaped around in my chest like a maniac. I was surprised by my fear. But Maggie said that she loved me and Kathleen said that I was brave. Stella didn't know how I could stand to talk about it at all and DeeDee flashed a look at me I couldn't fathom and bit her lip.

Maggie came next in the circle. "I wasn't molested but I can remember Dad kissing me. Yuck! His mouth was always open and all that spit! Mother made me do something when I was seven or eight." Her voice trembled and faded. "She made me drown a kitten in a fruit jar because we had too many." She rose up with her chin high, fighting back tears. She stood before us and Kathleen took her hand and told her about loving her. Stella grumbled about Maggie being great and DeeDee added that she was wonderful. I told her that I had "forgotten" about those openmouthed kisses. I thanked her for having the courage to remember.

It was Kathleen's turn now and in her measured tones she said, "Well, I remember those kisses, too." She shrugged. "But I wasn't molested that I know of. I don't have much to say, really, because nothing much happened." We made the best we could out of this dry confession and I wondered how Kathleen could stand being with us mere mortals and our tawdry little problems.

When DeeDee's time came, I realized that we had managed to do this in birth order without planning it. I studied DeeDee. Something was going on but I didn't know what it was, and besides, Stella's turn would be next and her pain, her need, her torment seemed so much greater than any of ours, that once again we allowed her to dominate us like some great thundercloud.

So DeeDee slid through the initiation, using Stella as camouflage. She admitted to the disgusting kisses bestowed upon us all by our father. She pointed out that in addition to spittle, there was a very large tongue and his breath was rank with smoke and booze. When she stood before me I said, "I love you." I looked deeply into her eyes. I searched for her soul. There was a moment of vulnerability and then a lightning strike of pure hatred. I shrank back but then it was gone and there was Stella waiting.

138

"I don't want to do this," she said. She scrunched back into the shadows, making herself smaller in her chair. We said nothing and waited. And then the rocking began, back and forth in the chair. Both of her hands went up to her face. One hand went over her forehead and the other over her mouth, and when she spoke we could see only her nose and glimpses of her upper lip and sometimes her eyes when her fingers slipped. The hands rested uneasily in opposite directions across her face. The hand over her mouth slipped and the words poured out, uttered in cracking, sobbing, choking sounds as though they were emerging from a pit beneath the earth. "When I was six or seven, maybe five, I found myself in the bathtub with all my clothes on. One of the voices told me to go there. I don't remember how I got there. He used to catch me in the bathroom, you know." A bright eye gleamed behind a finger.

When she rocked forward again she added from behind closed fingers and clenched teeth, "It was hard to pee when Bri was around putting his fingers in me." Her body trembled with the contradiction of two powerful compulsions. Revelation and secrecy. "Mother saw once! And I yelled at her. He makes me do it in the bathroom! And do you know what she did? Do you? Do you?"

But we were like witnesses frozen before a natural catastrophe beyond our puny imaginations. Stella's masks were stripped away and underneath was an abyss. Her face was split and grinding against itself in the way that the plates of hardened rock must shift and shriek against itself when molten lava pushes upward. She held onto herself as though she would break in two.

"She told him to cut it out and then she looked at me and said, 'You try to get along with your brother.' And he was thirteen or fourteen then and he just smiled and smiled."

The quaking stopped. Her hands fell away from her face and she slumped forward in the padded vinyl-covered chair.

139

Kathleen helped her to stand and stumble from sister to sister asking us what we thought of her now that we had heard her story. Maybe we shouldn't have done it because now she saw the horror in our eyes. She saw that we knew her truly now. We had seen her secret inner life. We knew who she was. She turned away and I never saw her again.

* * * * *

The next morning I drove across town and picked up Lily to take her to brunch. Stella was inside me somewhere throbbing like a toothache. I could see that Lily was nervous because she stumbled a little getting into my brand new Honda. She said nothing about my new car. She gave me directions to the restaurant and while we waited for the light to change I impulsively blurted, "You know, Mother, I love you. I really do love you." It came from my heart as innocently as a blade of new grass.

She recoiled from my upraised hand. "Don't get carried away with that love stuff!" She was wretched, shrunken, small. She huddled in the corner of the passenger seat unable to give or receive love.

A cold pity passed through me in one long shudder. There was nothing I could do about this. Ever.

We had our brunch. She had a Denver omelet. I had scrambled eggs and hash browns. I said, "You know I've been in therapy."

"Yes," she replied sullenly, pushing her eggs around with a fork.

"I need to talk to you about it."

"What for?"

"It's thirty-two years of my life. And yours. It's important."

"I don't think about it."

"Thirty-two years? You just ignore them, don't think about them or remember them?"

"No."

"No?"

"I have put the past behind me and I don't want to talk about it." She took a bite of the omelet and looked me in the eye.

I remembered Elaine and her mother. I took a deep breath. "Okay, let the past go. What I am talking to you about today is whether or not you want to have a relationship with me."

She stopped chewing.

"I want two things. I want you to stop talking to me about your sex life. It offends me. Secondly, I want you to acknowledge my existence. I get more compliments from perfect strangers than I have ever gotten from you."

She swallowed the bite. "I'm just not the type to gush over people." She patted at her mouth with a napkin.

"Mother, there's a difference between gushing over people and acknowledging the existence of your oldest daughter."

"I told Kathleen that I like your new hairstyle," she offered reluctantly.

Painfully, I realized that she didn't want to experience me as myself. To acknowledge me as a feeling, sentient being. "Don't tell Kathleen, tell me!" I demanded.

She sat silent.

"Try!"

"I like your blouse," she muttered to her plate of ruined eggs.

Sartre's impenetrable tome *Being and Nothingness* finally made sense to me. It explained my crime against my mother. I was stuck with having a body with feelings and having to sleep and eat and touch but at the same time I experienced myself as nothing. As though having my body and my feelings and my breath and my clitoris and my ears didn't matter at all. And if I asserted that stuff of my being, I betrayed my very nature

141

which was nothing. And so it went, round and round. What I
wanted from her and what I had always wanted from her was
some acknowledgment that my beingness mattered. That my
beingness was not a violation of some sort. What sort, I was
never sure. The space I occupied? The air I breathed? She
couldn't acknowledge me. She acknowledged my blouse.

I was gasping with the truth of this when she insisted that
we drive to the Colorado River for a walk. She took her
revenge on me there by striding quickly down a path familiar
to her but unknown to me and I trotted after her, ridiculous in
a pair of high-heeled shoes. This was my punishment for being
in drag to please my mother, who could not be pleased. And
yet it was fitting that I, who had shoes for every occasion, had
lost my ability to follow my mother.

When she shut her tight, grim lips down over a new story
about a new man she had met at the senior citizens' dance,
I decided that I would take it. The compliment about my
blouse and her shut mouth.

9

I rushed back to Los Angeles and impatiently waited for Tuesday night to roll around so that I could report my results to Elaine. But she wasn't there. "Where is she?" I demanded of Deanna.

"Elaine's mother died, Annie."

"Is Elaine coming back?"

"I don't think so."

I called Elaine at home that night. "Elaine, I miss you and I'm so sorry about your mother. Are you okay?"

"I don't want to talk about it."

I was taken aback by her bitter voice. I gulped. "I wanted to tell you how important you are to me. The example you set for me helped me in Boulder City. I saw Lily, my mother, without flinching and I stood up to her. I. . . ."

But she interrupted me rudely, "I don't want to talk about this with you."

"But Elaine, are you coming back?"

"No." And she hung up.

"I admire you and love you, and I thank you," I said to the dial tone.

* * * * *

Father's Day follows fast upon Mother's Day and since I had actually passed through Mother's Day without being stoned, shut down or numb, I decided to tackle Father's Day as well. "I may even be able to handle all holidays," I announced optimistically to the group. "I'm planning Christmas now."

"In June?" asked Susana.

"Yes, I want to go back to Storm Lake. I haven't been back in ten years or more. Maybe Thanksgiving instead of Christmas, I don't know yet."

"In the meantime, what about your father?" Kelly flung her purse at the floor and sat down. She was late, as usual.

"I've got a letter. So there!" I retorted.

"Well, I don't!" she said defiantly to Deanna.

"Why are you wearing only one shoe?" asked Susana.

Kelly looked down at her foot covered with a red wool sock. "Now I have gout! Can you believe it? Stress, the doctors say."

"Why didn't you write your father letter, Kelly?" Deanna's face was set in stern lines which marred her perfect lipstick.

Kelly exploded. "I've had it! Just had it with all of this. I'm leaving. Leaving for good. Just like Elaine." She gathered herself together and limped out of the room, banging the door as she left.

"We're small tonight," Deanna commented dryly into the shocked stillness. Elaine was gone. Susana was about to graduate. Marsha rarely spoke. Melanie had a work deadline to meet and she was absent. Christina had a letter written and so did I.

Susana broke the silence. "This seems to be a night about leaving the group, so I guess I'll start. Deanna and I have talked about this and we agree that it's time now for me to go on to marriage counseling with my husband. I'm pretty much done with the incest stuff."

"Now you have more counseling to do?" I was depressed by this. I still wanted a quick fix.

Susana laughed. "Look at it this way, Annie. I spent six years in therapy getting nowhere until now. This took a year and a half. Marriage counseling will be a piece of cake." She waited for me to smile back at her. Reluctantly, I did. "Now, do you want me to tell you about my visit to my grandfather's grave?"

I admitted I did. I admitted I didn't want her to go and leave me. I admitted I would miss her. "Who will hand out tissues?" I blurted nervously.

"We'll give the job to Melanie," Kelly announced, standing at the door. Her dark hair had escaped its pins as usual. "Can I come back?"

We all turned to look at her.

"Well, group, shall we let her in?" Deanna settled herself into her throne with great satisfaction. A collective sigh escaped and we gathered her into us. Maybe everybody wasn't leaving.

"Susana? You were saying?" Deanna pointedly remarked.

"Before I was so rudely interrupted, you mean?"

Kelly laughed at us.

"I went to my grandfather's grave and I sat on his tombstone and I read that letter to him. The one you all liked so much." She laughed out loud. "I wonder what the old bastard thought about that!" She stretched her plump arms above her head. "God, but it felt good and it still does." She reached behind the sofa and lifted up a cake box. "So in honor of my last night, I've brought black-out cake and champagne." She put her booty on the square coffee table. "And apple juice for the non-drinkers too." She pushed the juice toward me.

We set about munching and sipping and when we were starting on our second pieces of cake and drink, Deanna insisted that we work. "Annie?"

So I read my Father Letter.

Father,
As an adult, I experience you with both indifference and dismay. My indifference arises from the curious biological fact that we are father and daughter, but never family to each other. Our relationship is that of tyrant to thing. You were the tyrant and I was the thing. I was your pet rock for television viewing. I was like all the other small animals in the house which you poked, pinched, slapped, and tortured. I was never a person to you and I was never your little girl. You were never a person to me and never my daddy.

When I was asked to make a list of five things I liked about my father, the only thing I had on my list was that I thought you were beautiful, handsome.

My dismay comes from the realization that in some way, I am not free of you yet.

Annie

"Boring!" said Kelly, stuffing her face with her third piece of cake.

"What are you hiding?" Susana asked with her new serenity.

"Another letter to your father, Annie." Deanna sipped her cider.

"I hope this isn't going to take as long as her mother thing." Kelly wiped crumbs from the corner of her mouth.

"And what is your problem anyway?" I was furious with her.

"Tell," Deanna mumbled, mouth full.

"I'm seeing my parents next week. With Deanna." All the fight went out of her.

"Aren't you ready?"

"Yes, I guess so but. . . ."

"You can do it. I did it and I didn't even have Deanna with me."

"I have my notes." She waved a sheaf of paper at me.

"Notes?"

Deanna said, "It's okay to have notes when you confront your parents. Kelly and I will give you all the news next week. Now everybody go home. You all have your assignments, right?"

"Right," I replied. Resistance was not only useless, it was stupid.

The sun flooded into my bedroom, waking me on Saturday morning. I snuggled luxuriously into the bedcovers, feeling relaxed and sexy. No deadlines to meet. Nowhere to go. I put my hand down between my legs and as my finger touched my clitoris, I saw my father. I sprang out of bed, shaking my fingers as though I had just been burned. "Fuck! Fuck! Fuck!" I muttered, washing my hands in the bathroom sink. I brushed my teeth and the letter composed itself. I dashed down to the kitchen table and wrote it out as fast as I could move my hand.

147

Father,

My therapist said that I should write you another letter. This pisses me off because I am sick to death of even giving you a thought, let alone an entire letter. What is there to say? You were an asshole. You molested me. You were never nice to me except when you were molesting me. I'm offended by Father's Day. What father?

You are my phantom sex partner who stimulates but never satisfies. You are there right before orgasm whether I give that pleasure to myself or with a lover. I hate you for that.

I hate you for making me share this with other people, even my therapy group. I hate you for all the orgasms I've lost forever. I hate you for the hatred I've expressed to the wrong people. I hate you for all the orgasms I've withheld from myself, from my lovers.

It was my only defense against you and now I don't know how to stop. You fuck head, bastard, child-molesting drunk! Most of all, I hate you for invading my most intimate private pleasures. How dare you?

Annie

"I'm so embarrassed," I whispered into the quiet which greeted this letter after I read it aloud. But Deanna was crossing the room to me and lifting me up. She took me to the front where the chairs had been cleared away. She handed me the bataca and the room receded from me with the walls running away from me at the speed of light, and everybody disappeared, and all I could remember thinking was: "Oh no! Not again!"

And sure enough, the next day my back muscles were excruciatingly tender to the touch and once more the purity of my rage had so drained me that I slept and slept. I dragged through the week like a wrung-out mop.

* * * * *

I continued to make money at an exploding rate. There didn't seem to be any obstacles in my path.

"She's about ready, don't you think?" Deanna made eye contact with each member of the group. "We agree, Annie. Just write a goodbye letter to your father and then graduation! Congratulations. You may have a ritual or a party if you wish. Invite Susana too." She sighed tiredly. It wasn't the perfectly groomed Deanna I was accustomed to seeing. Her lipstick was smeared onto her even white teeth.

"What happened to you?" I didn't want to deal with graduating just yet but excitement was bubbling happily in my stomach.

"Kelly and I just finished up the session with her parents and I feel as though I've been battered myself."

Kelly hung on every word Deanna spoke like a barnacle on a hull, then she ran her hand through her hair using her fingers as a comb. "I see that I will have to give them both up if I ever want a normal life for myself. I'm too tired to cry about it." She paused. "I'm not crazy. That's the best part. I'm not crazy. They denied everything."

"You're not crazy at all, Kelly. They are." Melanie handed Kelly the tissue box and then Kelly cried. After the sobs subsided, Melanie took a check from her purse. "This, my friends, is a check for two thousand three hundred and twelve dollars. That is the exact amount incest therapy has cost me, as of today. I am looking at new cars. Kelly, what about Volvos?"

"Cost a lot more than two thousand bucks," she snuffled.

"You got that from your parents?"

"Yes, and I have other money of my own to go with this."

"Maybe I'll ask my parents for money, too. I bet I've spent over three thousand so far, and that doesn't count all the other stuff I've done trying to not be crazy." She retreated into mental calculations.

"What about you, Annie?" asked Deanna.

Melanie joined in. "Yeah, Annie, why don't you get some money from your parents? They owe you."

I shrugged. "My Mother is on social security and my father is a hopeless drunk with no money."

"Oh yeah, I keep forgetting. Your father is basically dead, isn't he?"

"What did you say?" I leaned forward urgently. "Repeat what you said, Melanie."

"I said that your father is basically dead."

"That's it! Thank you."

"For what?"

"I'll tell you next week when I read my final letter and we have the party."

I drove home happily because that was it. She was absolutely, perfectly, one thousand percent correct. I had been confused. Susana's grandfather was dead, so she could sit on his grave and yell at him. Melanie's father was alive, so she could get him to pay for her therapy. My father, on the other hand, was neither alive nor dead and this was what had been confusing me. I wrote:

Father,

Now that I understand you are basically dead, I can say goodbye. It has been your in-between state which bewildered me.

I know that the worst thing in the world is to not have feelings. To be dead and cold inside, not feeling anything at all.

Goodbye,
Annie

As I read the word "goodbye" in my last night of incest therapy, I unscrewed the cap of the whiskey bottle. The chip of dried ice I had so carefully purchased for one dollar fizzed up into a grey fog in the water of the half-empty bottle and slowly vanished into the air. Kelly and Marsha, Melanie and Christina, Susana and Deanna and I held hands in a circle as we watched the essence of my father fade away into nothingness. The nothingness he had chosen for himself. "Goodbye," we said. "Goodbye."

* * * * *

With Tuesday nights no longer dominating my life, I was at loose ends. I cast about for another activity. Acting classes, painting—writing?

Over the next few months I planned my holiday season. I saw Deanna from time to time and learned to give myself pleasure without the phantom images of my father intruding upon me. Life beat on and a tide of well-being grew within me. There were entire days in a row without guilt. When the guilt was there, I was no longer its prisoner. I laughed at it and I used my affirmation. "I am innocent and I forgive myself completely." I bought the condominium in Pacific Palisades. Life was good and getting better.

One hot August afternoon, the telephone rang. It was Kathleen. "Hi, I hear you're planning your holidays already."

"True, true," I replied comfortably. "I don't want to be lost in space this year like Christmas every year before this."

"Well, why don't you come here?"

"But I've planned to go to Storm Lake."

"There'll be skiing here and we'll have a good time. Mother won't be here. She'll be in Storm Lake."

"Storm Lake?" I echoed.

"Yes, she's going there to visit Kevin."

"Kevin?"

Kathleen sighed. I could not be diverted. "She told me she hasn't talked to the boys about any of this and she wants to hear their side."

"I see. Let me get this straight. I've just done fifty-seven of the most difficult nights of my life to turn myself inside out and get well. Stella's crazy. DeeDee is something—I don't know what. Maggie's not so happy and Lily is going to go see Kevin?"

"Yes."

"She's never visited him before."

"I know."

A mutual silence prevailed.

She repeated her invitation. "Come be with us, Annie."

After I hung up, I contemplated the threads on the edge of the overstuffed chair for an hour. I called DeeDee in Storm Lake. "What's this I hear about Mother coming out there to see Kevin at Christmas?"

"Oh, you heard."

"I just talked to Kathleen."

"Did you know she was really upset when she found out you were planning to come here?"

"Oh? What did she say?"

"That you've spoiled a lot of holidays and she didn't want you spoiling this one too."

"I guess I have, haven't I?" I said ironically. My child's heart noted that my mother did not want to be in the same town with me for Christmas. "You know what?"

"What?"

"She thinks I did it."

"Did what?"

"She thinks I caused all this and she will never forgive me for it." I was finally at the bottom.

DeeDee groaned. "Well, what are you going to do about it?"

"I don't know. I have to think this over." I put the receiver back in the cradle and faced Lily's silence for the first time. She had not contacted me since Mother's Day. She had not even sent me one of her ubiquitous greeting cards for the 4th of July.

I reached Maggie the next morning. "Annie, I'm sure she doesn't mean anything by it."

"She doesn't want to even be in the same town with me, Maggie." I could feel Lily's tracks on Maggie like the tracing of snail slime on a sidewalk. Maggie, DeeDee, and Kathleen. There was a new distance between us.

That night the dream came to me in color, vividly etched. Bri sat at a table, in a room filled with evil which corrodes the human soul with its sheer bleakness. The table was the kind that sits in a room where prisoners are brought. A table top fit for an inquisitor's outer chamber. It was the only piece of furniture in the room, except, of course, for the chair where the inquisitor, Brian, Jr., sat. It was a table where knives have been. A table scarred with despair and mindless boredom. Knives thrown into its wooden flesh.

I have been brought before him to empty my things out onto that table top but I am not afraid because I am there on a mission. I am a commando, a fighter. I empty out my bag. Many things tumble out but all that matters is the brown bread. Other prisoners rush up. They are my sisters. They grab the chunks of the good brown bread off that terrible surface: "Brown bread, brown bread, we never get brown bread." They push it into their mouths with both hands. Stella isn't there.

Bri ignores them. He keeps his eyes on me. He smiles charmingly but I am not fooled. I am past that. I can no longer believe he is just a man with a job to do. Even so, I shiver because I now know the whole of his corruption and how deep it runs. Knowing this is the only way I can survive. I keep my eyes on his and I see he thinks himself still in power and he has not yet understood that I have slipped through. That I am

153

free. That it does not matter that I am in the house of the Tyrant. There is no longer any way to hold me, or kill me, or keep me. I can come and go as I please. I am in the house of the tyrant because I choose to be there. I am on a mission.

My mission is to find my daughter. I go to the telephone to call her but my sisters crowd around me. "No, no. She controls all communication." They mean the Tyrant. The Tyrant controls all communication and they are right. All the telephones are nailed to the wall and the dials have been removed. Calls come in, but none go out.

I shrug and turn my back on Bri. I know he is only a lieutenant. I go out to the shed in the back and there she is. The Tyrant. My mother. I walk up behind her as easy as a cat burglar and I twist her arm behind her back. I announce to the rows and rows and rows of oppressed workers sitting before her in the food processing shed, "If anybody moves, I'll bite her ear off." Nobody moves.

I woke. My teeth were too big and I felt the shape of an ear in that space in my mouth as though I had put my mouth around her left ear, but I had not yet bitten down and torn it off in one terrible ripping with my big teeth. Instead, the ear shape hovered there in my mouth and I shuddered at the near feel of it on my palate and tongue, but I knew that if anyone had moved, I would have done it. Taken that ear. Bitten it. Torn it off her head and eaten it. Blood and all. But nobody moved. Not even her henchman. My brother, Brian, Jr.

The ghostly ear and my powerful, too-big teeth were my companions as I sat at the kitchen table and wrote my final letter.

Mother,
I want you to know that I find you and your actions despicable. Using my sisters to express your unrelenting hostility toward me is the action of a coward.

154

Denying the facts of incest, rape and molestation in our family is complete and total selfishness on your part.

Aligning yourself with child molesters, rapists and wife batterers makes you a traitor to all of the innocent people who have suffered so much, and there are so many of us.

I wash my hands of you. I will no longer contribute to your financial support and I will no longer communicate with you in writing or by telephone or on any holiday of any sort.

Your behavior makes me believe the very worst of you which is that you are a child molester yourself.

Goodbye,
Annie

After I wrote it I drove to my office and ran off seven copies. I prepared seven envelopes and I mailed them. The original went to Lily and the other six went to my sisters and brothers. Then I went home to call my sisters. I got DeeDee first. I read the letter to her.

"No! Annie! No, No." And then she wept.

I called Kathleen and she said, "Do you have to do this?"

"Yes," I replied.

Maggie said, "I'm so confused. Are you sure?"

"Yes," I said.

DeeDee called me back the next morning and without preamble, announced, "I'm coming to Los Angeles. Will you pick me up at LAX at seven? Maggie's coming in at seven-thirty. I'll be at Northwest and Maggie at the Western Terminal."

I was dumbfounded.

"Well, will you pick us up?" she asked impatiently.

"Yeah," I said, jerking out of my shock. "Sure, I'll be there."

155

I hung up and stared at the telephone. This meant I would not be alone when the letter hit the family. Perhaps I would not be an orphan after all. Perhaps I would end up with somebody unlike Elaine who had lost everyone. Or Kelly who had no one, not even her sister who refused to believe her story.

DeeDee wanted to go straight to the beach. "But it will be dark by the time we get there," I protested.

"I don't care," she retorted.

I took them to Malibu where the creek runs down to the sea. DeeDee walked directly to the crashing waves without looking to the right or the left and without speaking to either Maggie or me. Like all land-locked creatures, she was starved for the open sea. She marched briskly along, picking through driftwood, pebbles, and shells while Maggie and I trailed behind her. The sky was blue-gray with hints of sunset stain barely visible on the horizon.

Maggie and I sat down in the sand and we removed our shoes and socks and waited for DeeDee. We were just there with each other. Maggie was like a candle flame with her red hair and her loving presence. We did not speak. Our attention was on DeeDee.

She finally came back. Her freckles were dark against her pale face. Her light brown hair was cut in bangs across her forehead. She stood over me. "I feel overwhelmed. Do I have to do what you are doing?"

"No," I told her.

She flashed a look of utter disbelief. "You're asking me to choose between Mother and you."

The salted sea air stung my eyes. Salted tears on my cheeks. I said, "I know it seems that way, DeeDee. But don't you see? That's the way it's set up. The way it's always been set up. I'm not the mother here. I'm one of you. I'm one of the kids. Mother and I are not equal. We are not the same person. It's a false choice."

156

"Umph!" she grunted and turned her back on me. "I'm ready to go now."

Stabbed, I turned to Maggie. "And what about you? What's your position on Mother, anyway?"

"I don't know. I'm so confused."

"I wish you'd stop saying that, Maggie." I took a deep breath. "You know what?"

"What?" she asked heavily, hunched in the sand in the gathering darkness.

"If I knew what your position was, I'd support it and you. Can you believe that?"

"I think so."

"I want the same from you."

We sat quietly for a moment watching DeeDee disappear into the darkness as she marched toward the parking lot. The set of her shoulders, the movement of her back communicated rage.

When I got them to the condo in Pacific Palisades, DeeDee raced up and down the three levels turning on all the lights. She whirled to face me. "You *are* a success, aren't you?"

"Yes, I guess I am."

"Doesn't make sense," she muttered.

I grabbed her arm and swung her around to me. "Oh yes it does. Resentment stops everything. Everything! Love, money, health, feelings. Until I faced the truth of my incest, I could not succeed. I could not let go of my anger."

She wrenched herself out of my grasp and ran upstairs to my bedroom. I found her rummaging in my closet. "Can I try this on?" She held up my red Norma Kamali dress with the shoulder pads.

I looked back at Maggie behind me. She raised her eyebrows indicating that she didn't know what was happening either. "Of course," I said soothingly.

157

She slipped the dress over her head and went to the bathroom which was covered with mirrors along one wall."Now what do you wear with this? I want all the accessories. Just like the picture." She referred to a photograph of myself I had sent for a Christmas gift the year before.

I brought her a black leather belt, jet beads and earrings, a black ceramic bracelet. "Sometimes I wear this too." I threw a black velvet prom cape over her shoulders. "For the theater or the ballet. I had it relined." I stroked the velvet. The cape was more than fifty years old. "I found it in an antique clothing store on Main Street in Santa Monica."

Maggie joined us and the three of us were reflected back to ourselves in the glittering mirrors under the overhead lights. "I want to look like you," DeeDee declared.

"You do?" I was appalled. Despite the mirrors I lived with, I had been avoiding them for months and months but now I looked. "I'm the image of Lily, aren't I?" I said finally.

It was true. More so than any of Lily's daughters. Her youthful self made manifest.

"How odd," I murmured.

DeeDee stormed out of the bathroom and threw the cape away from her. It swirled in a great dark arc above the white carpeted bedroom floor and landed in an inky crumpled heap at the foot of the bed. A coyote howled in the starry night beyond the open doors of the bedroom balcony. DeeDee paced the room. Maggie and I stood in the doorway of the bathroom jammed together. She threw herself at the bed. The full skirts of the red dress swirled around her full body. She was face down in the pillows.

I let the silence build. Build and swell until something happened. Maggie opened her mouth to speak but I silenced her with a frown and a gesture. The tension grew as the feeling expanded. Maggie and I hung on the outer edges of this expanding bubble which billowed out from the bed where

158

DeeDee lay. We hovered on its borders but Maggie could endure it no longer. "Would you two *do* something? This feels really bad."

I exploded. My shout lifted the hair up on the back of my neck like a sudden blast of wind or maybe a flash fire. "I AM NOT MOTHER. I AM NOT MOTHER. I AM NOT MOTHER."

At the third shout, Maggie whimpered, "Annie, Annie...."

And then the three of us were on the floor together. DeeDee on her belly while Maggie brought blankets and pillows, tucking them all around DeeDee. Pulling the bed covers down off the bed as fast as she could. I lowered DeeDee to the floor. She trembled and shook.

"What happened to you, honey?" I asked as gently as I could.

"I can only sleep on my stomach," she mumbled into the pillows. But Maggie and I heard because we were down there in the pillows with her, listening.

"Why is that?" I asked, carefully removing the jet beads from around her neck. Maggie stroked the nape of her neck.

"Because one night I woke up and he had taken all my clothes off. I slept on my back in those days." She squeezed herself deeper into the pillows.

"He had no right to do that to you, DeeDee." I wondered if she could breathe down there.

"He, who?" Maggie searched all around the room wildly.

But I already knew. DeeDee put the pillows up around her ears. I slipped the wire loops of the earrings out of her lobes. I raised my eyes to Maggie and saw that she was filled with a raw and uncertain agony.

"Bri?" she whispered. "Bri?" She looked down at DeeDee who had drawn her knees up to her stomach.

I put the jewelry in a little heap on the night table. "That's right," I affirmed.

"That bastard! He should be killed!"

I was shocked by the vengeance in Maggie's once innocent blue eyes. "Yeah," I said heavily. "I've thought about it but I can't figure out how to kill him without killing him, or how to have him killed without being responsible. Or worse, being like him."

We were locked together in the quandary when DeeDee stirred beneath our hands and we let it go and turned toward our little sister.

Maggie took up my refrain. "He had no right, DeeDee. No right." I repeated the words, "No right, no right."

Maggie again and then me and the words fell into a somber cadence. DeeDee lifted her head out of the pillows to ask in a little girl voice, "Really?"

"Really!" I said firmly and added, "That fuckhead, bastard, slimebag, pussball! He had no right!" I ran out of names and I signalled Maggie for help.

"That pig bastard ought to be hung by the balls and left there to rot," she vehemently contributed.

This reminded me of a curse I had always wanted to use. "May he boil in shit forever."

With that, DeeDee sat up smiling. Mascara ran down her cheeks in black wavy lines. "I love it." She paused. "He had no right?"

Maggie and I came in together on cue: "He had no right!"

"I was flattered, you know. He started paying attention to me. At first. . . ." She stopped and we thought she was going to take another dive into the pillows.

But quickly I asked, "How old were you when it started?"

She straightened. "Seven or eight, maybe?" Panic swept across her face and she rubbed her cheeks. Now she had black smudges beneath each eye like a football player.

"Hey, it's okay," I said. "Most of us incest kids don't remember much about our childhood. Even Maggie doesn't

160

remember much and that's just because she was around. Huh, Maggie?"

Maggie nodded energetically. "I bet you'd have walked across broken glass for him, wouldn't you?"

She turned to Maggie in amazed relief. "My big brother paying attention to me. I was so lonely." Maggie pushed a strand of hair away from DeeDee's dirty face. "That's why Stella's been so mad at me and me at her. He'd get Stella and me together and we played this game. It was called the blanket game. We'd lay on either side of him and he'd roll us up in the blankets and feel us up. After a while I didn't want to do it any more, but I knew Stella was doing it because she always had candy and comic books and toys. He paid her. . . ."

She stopped breathing. "I'm so ashamed." Her face broke into pieces as the reflection of the moon does in the water when a pebble strikes it; the silvery disk gleaming and rippling and then flowing back together. She came back and cried out, "Oh help me. Help me! I was jealous. Jealous of Stella and I couldn't forgive her."

Maggie and I held her and we stroked and cooed and gentled her until she calmed under our hands. "You deserve love too. It's okay." There was no hurry now and so we moved downstairs and lit the fire. We brought the bedding and the pillows and then DeeDee slowly down the staircase in an unwieldy lump. Maggie and I took turns running errands. DeeDee was never alone.

We cuddled together watching the flames leap in the fireplace and after a long quiet I said, "And what else?"

She was too tired to resist. "I'm like you, Annie. I know it all. Forever. I knew Kevin molested her too. And paid her." She sighed and rested her head on my shoulder. "And I was the first one to see Kevin after he was assaulted in the park by that teenage boy, remember?"

"I remember," said Maggie. "Kevin didn't know about erections. He thought the boy had peed on him."

161

Bitterly, DeeDee agreed. "I was walking home from school and Kevin came running up to me and I knew. I knew immediately what happened. I took care of him. Isn't that wild? I was nine and he was eight."

"So that's why Kevin told you about his molesting Audrey?" Maggie fit another piece of the puzzle together and I wondered for the one-hundredth time if there was to be an end to this nightmare ever.

DeeDee bowed her head and I perceived the yoke about her neck and shoulders. The burden she had been carrying all these years alone. Stella's secret. Brian's secret. Kevin's secret. Her secret. "The weird thing is," she muttered faintly, "I don't think Stella remembers about me. At least not consciously."

And then Maggie voiced what I had been thinking. "Did you tell Mother?"

"When I was nine. I remember telling her about Bri, Stella and me." Her voice was dreamy, distant.

"What did she say?" Maggie leaned forward eagerly.

"I don't remember." A tear slid softly through her lower lashes making a track in the black smudge on her cheek.

"I call that the Lily Effect, myself." I prodded a log with the poker and the flames shot up.

"The what?" Maggie asked.

"The Lily Effect. It's like my dream. One way communication. Instead of Big Brother and the Thought Police, we have Big Mother and the Thought Police." I pulled the screen across the fireplace pit. "When you talk to Lily sometimes, doesn't it feel as though your words have fallen into a black hole never to be seen or heard again?"

While DeeDee thought that over, Maggie asked herself a question and answered it. "And where was Dad while all of this was going on? Away. And when he was home, drunk. Sticking his tongue in everybody's mouth."

We put our arms around each other and pondered the ruin of our family like survivors sitting on a hillside overlooking a city leveled by a bomb.

The next day DeeDee went back to Storm Lake and found a therapist in Milwaukee.

The letter had been delivered; I went about my life and wondered what would happen next. It turned out to be Kevin.

I recognized his voice at once, even though I had not spoken to him in years. His voice had the oily charm of all the men in the Malloy family and I heard lies running through his speaking. "When I got the letter you wrote to Mother, I crumpled it up and I threw it away. I thought it was bullshit." He stopped.

"And?" I wasn't about to help him. I held tightly to the receiver.

"And then I couldn't stop thinking about it and so I took it out of the trash."

"Yeah, so?"

"I didn't ever beat up my wife, you know."

"I know."

"You're talking about Bri, there?"

"Right." Then I remembered the night Kevin had come to my apartment in Los Angeles for comfort because there was blood on the walls and holes in the bathroom door where Bri had punched through in one of his attacks on his tiny ex-wife, Rita. Kevin had left Los Angeles to return to the home town of Storm Lake after that.

"Well, I didn't," he insisted.

"I know," I repeated.

He suddenly veered in another direction. "Why shouldn't Mother visit me?"

"She's never done it before, has she?" I understood everything.

"No, he said in a little hurt voice.

"She's using you, Kevin."

163

"Using me?"

"Yes, to justify her actions. To find a defense. Are you going to let her do it?"

"I don't know. I'm not sure I understand."

I wanted to have hope. I wanted to believe he could change. I wanted to have a brother who could be whole. "It's good you called. It makes me think something might be possible for you and me. All of us. Are you in therapy?"

"Not anymore."

"Why not?"

Silence.

I heard him gulp. He said, "I want to tell you something, but you must promise not to tell anyone."

Even as I said, "What?" I was cursing myself. Did I need to know more?

"Promise?" he repeated.

"Promise." I waited for the blow.

"I go to the park."

"Yes."

"I expose myself to the kids."

Tiredly, I used the old routine. "When did it start?"

"After I stopped with Audrey."

Lie! I thought. "How often?" I said.

"It varies," he said. Now his voice became full and heavy. Engorged. There was pain in it. "I play a game with myself. I drive home different ways but the park is on the way by Edward Lake. Sometimes I can hold off for as much as two weeks."

"Is there a time of the day?"

"Oh sure. The hardest time is between five and five-thirty in the afternoon, Monday through Friday."

"Why is that?"

"Because Josie doesn't get home until then. I have that half hour to myself."

A prickle of fear danced up my spine like a spider. "You mean you think about it all of the time?"

"Yes."

"And when you do it, how does it feel?"

"Feel?" he said sleepily and suddenly my cursed imagination transported me to the familiar park of my teenage years and I'm there with him under the maple trees on the green rolling lawns. My vision shifts to his hands fumbling at his fly as he stands on the edges looking on to the children on the jungle gym. He reaches for his penis which stiffens under the beer belly which he has grown to hide himself from himself. I feel him hoping and not hoping that one child will turn and see that sperm shooting and then shaking off that deflating lump of flesh. The betrayer. He stuffs it back into that place behind the zipper and the cotton flap of his briefs. He is still hungry.

I shook off my vision and repeated my question.

"Feel? Oh, angry. Real, real mad. Furious."

I flinched. I knew just what he meant. The hatred rising up all twisted around the heat in the loins, flashing through the body with a thrill of release but as the orgasm passes through it leaves a stain of remorse and guilt. We shared an emotional/sexual landscape, victim and oppressor alike.

"But you go back? Again and again."

"Yeah."

"Addiction. Like heroin. You get a rush. You know it's bad and it causes you pain but you can't let go."

"Right!" He was pleased that I understood.

I wasn't pleased. I sent a silent prayer to DeeDee: "He's so heavy, how could you stand it?" I knew she had decided to stop interacting with him until she sorted herself out and now I knew why. I plunged on. "Doesn't this have to do with when you were assaulted?"

The air froze. I thought the telephone wires would snap. He whispered to me, "I hate white tennis shoes."

"Tennis shoes?"

"He wore white tennis shoes and glasses and a blue windbreaker. I hate anybody who wears those things and looks like him."

"But, Kevin," I said, "aren't you like him yourself? Haven't you become him?"

He ignored my question. "He was never found, never punished."

"So if you get caught, he'll be punished?"

"Well, I'm not sure."

"I can't help you."

"What?"

I heard the whine in his voice. I laughed a little. He had called me because DeeDee had cut him off. "I'm not keeping my promise either, unless you call Maggie and tell her this and unless you immediately get into therapy with somebody who is an expert in these things."

He sputtered and whined.

"You're too much. And you stay away from DeeDee too. It's very simple, Kevin. The price of a relationship with me is mental health, integrity. Got it? This stuff in the park has got to stop. Now. All of it must stop. Now."

I didn't listen to his protests. I hung up and put my head between my legs until my eyesight cleared and my stomach stopped boiling.

10

In the following weeks I learned to eye my mailbox morosely. Letters were flying through the family in a blizzard. None were addressed to me. They were all copies. The first set had been mailed by Maggie to all family members.

Dear Brian,
   We are all victims of incest and I am concerned about what you are doing about it. My fears are for your children, Carrie and Billy. If they don't receive treatment then we must fear that Billy will become a perpetrator, and Carrie, a destroyed person.
   I am angry with myself for being so pleasant with you the last time I saw you. Talking to you as though

nothing had happened. I feel cheated. I was just getting to know you when all this broke open.

Maggie

She enclosed his response.

Maggie,

Are you going through a mid-life crisis or something? After getting nothing but Christmas cards from you for years, I suddenly get this letter. Assuming that you are of sound mind, I reject it and you.

I resent your interference in my relationship with my children. As for getting help, we got help long before any of you knew about this.

As for you being pleasant to me, since I would not ask you to make a sacrifice again, I hereby disown you as a sister. Now you are free to be any sort of asshole you care to be.

I also have no intentions of explaining my behavior to you or to throw myself on the mercy of a kangaroo court set up by my so-called loving sisters.

Carrie loves me. The following lines are extracted from a birthday card she sent me a few weeks ago:

Dearest Father,

I hope you have a wonderful birthday as you surely deserve it. Thanks for supporting me. I wouldn't be having such a good time if it weren't for you!

Love always,
Carrie

These lines reflect a relationship that has never

been better. The same is true of my son. Don't bother
me or mine again.

Brian

And then there was nothing in the mailbox for fourteen
entire days. There were no telephone calls. On the fifteenth
day, there was a thick packet waiting for me when I got home.
I looked at the return address. It was from Stella. I took a firm
grip on the metaphorical railing of my front row seat. I took a
ruler to read her letter and I rested my heart on its metal edge
for comfort. There were no paragraphs. Just one long rush of
words. I have separated them from each other but I cannot
decide which is worse, the words in one huge torrent or neat
paragraphs easy to read, easy to understand.

Brian,
    Your letter to Maggie was an absolute nightmare
to me. You have never experienced any consequences
for your actions and therefore it's really easy for you
to justify your behavior and escape from it.
    I've been getting help too and when they ask me
how I feel about you, I say that I like my brother because he is so intelligent. I enjoy my conversations
with him, his objective way of looking at things, his
PhD and his law degrees. And they ask me again and
again how I feel about you and I say that you were a
child too and that you had a hunger for closeness,
belonging, and intimacy. I excuse you for what you did
to me.
    You bastard! You produce and create guilt in your
victims and that's how you free yourself. You say:
"You want it as much as I do." Or, "Please, I need

you." And then you beg us, me and Carrie, to keep it a secret.

Carrie loves you? Is that what you think? I was a cheap fuck. A quarter here and there. A comic book, a piece of candy. Carrie's holding you up for an entire expensive private education and don't you forget it for a minute!

I ran away and you would bring me back home and Mother would say, "Retarded, that's what she is." I used to pull my own hair and slap myself and Mother would go and get me vitamins and say, "Take your happy pill."

I take lots of happy pills these days and I drink too. Thanks to you, I can't have sex unless I'm drunk.

I know everything. About how you tried to get your son and daughter into three-way sex with you and how you tried to get Carrie's girlfriends to have sex with you and no wonder she doesn't have any friends.

I know all about you. Forget the kangaroo court of your sisters. Remember me. I judge you and I pronounce you guilty. You are a total failure as a man, a parent, and a human being.

Love always,
Stella

I called Maggie. "Did you get Stella's letter?"

"I can't talk about it. I just can't stand it! And Kevin too!" But she didn't hang up.

"We're near the end, Maggie. We must have most of it now. Don't you think?"

"Who wanted to know it in the first place?" she said bitterly.

"You've got that right. I'll see you in Storm Lake for Thanksgiving?"

"You're going then instead of Christmas?"

170

"Yes, I have no desire to see Lily." I paused. "I love you Maggie, remember that. You decide what you need to do about her. This is not a contest between me and Lily. Okay?"

"Okay," she responded doubtfully.

I was about to hang up when she cleared her throat. "I talked to Stella."

"And?"

"She said that Mother went to see Brian two days ago."

"She was here in Los Angeles?" Brian lived twenty minutes drive from my door.

Maggie rushed pass this comment, adding, "And she told Stella that Brian had read her letter. He gave Mother a message to give to Stella."

She stopped talking for so long that I thought we had been disconnected. "Maggie? Maggie? Are you there?"

"Yeah, I'm here."

"What was the message?"

"He told Mother to tell Stella he was really glad she got that off her chest and that he knew she needed to do it."

"Damn, but he's good, isn't he?"

"There's more. He also asked for another copy of the letter since he's misplaced the original."

"Stella told you this? How is she?"

"I don't know. Weird. She had a fight with her therapist and said she won't go anymore."

We sighed together. "We can't save her, Maggie."

"I think I'm beginning to understand that."

I was now alert to her silences, her unspoken words. "And?"

"I talked to Mother too. Why do you call her Lily? It makes me nervous."

"Makes me nervous too but she's not my mother, is she?"

"This is so hard, Annie!"

"Spill it!"

"She said—" Maggie recreated Lily's voice, "I don't know why you girls are so upset. This has been going on for thousands of years all over the world." The tone was bright like a splinter of glass twinkling in sunshine.

"She said that?"

"She did."

And so I gave up Lily forever.

* * * * *

When the telephone rang again, I wanted to disconnect it permanently, but I trudged to it anyway. It was Laura. "You're in town?"

"Yes," she replied in her low musical voice. "I have a little time. Betty's gone off to see her parents for a few hours. Do you want to take a walk on the boardwalk like the good old days?"

"How's Betty?" I asked with difficulty.

I was rewarded with a warm response. I was learning. "Oh, she's just great! We got a new apartment and she has a new job and we are doing really well."

"I'm glad you're happy," I managed to gasp, and when I got past my jealousy, I found that I meant it. "I'll meet you at Small World Bookstore in twenty minutes."

When I arrived the sun had gone and the sky was streaked with gray and darkest pinks. Stars were coming out and the city lights glowed on the curve of the shoreline. I told her about Lily.

"Wow!" she said and put her arm around my waist. "Lots of things make more sense to me now. About us, I mean."

I settled my arm around her happily and we moved closer together in a comfortable puppy friendliness. "You have a wacky mother too. Sometimes I think there were at least four people in bed with us. Probably more."

"A veritable crowd," she agreed, laughing. She was still tall and golden. "How do you feel now that you've fired her?"

"Real, I feel real. I exist now. I'm not just a screen for Lily's projections. Do you know what I mean?" I looked over anxiously.

"Go on," she encouraged.

I saw that I was still attracted by Laura's lower lip. "I was so hurt and so puzzled. Why couldn't she reach out to me? After all, wasn't I her child? But the answer is, I'm not Lily's child. I'm her projection of herself. Particularly those parts of herself she cannot endure." We moved along slowly, hip to hip in step. "It's a simple story actually. She married my father because she was pregnant with me and because she wanted to rebel against her mother. A common thing, huh?" I stopped to face Laura.

She laughed out loud. "How well I know. You know very well I did it myself a thousand years ago."

"But remember what happened to Lily. Her mother up and died on her four days after I was born."

"Oh, yes." Laura breathed it out in the gathering dark.

"Yes. And then I think she looked at me and thought if it hadn't been for you my mother would still be alive." We walked quietly. "And then her mother turned out to be right about the marriage. They were totally unsuited to each other. So I figure, she looked to me again and blamed me for the marriage as well."

The darkness settled over the sea where the city lights could not reach. We strolled on the path between light and dark. Laura pulled me closer to her fullness. My awareness peacefully expanded into the night sky, to the vastness of the ocean horizon to the immensity of planetary space. Beyond that I knew there was galaxy upon galaxy into infinity. Lily's guilt and Lily's frozen hatred sped out into the void where it would travel forever like the last light from a star gone nova. It was free to go now because I wasn't standing in front of it

173

anymore. I had stepped aside. "She doesn't even know I've gone," I whispered. "It's such a habit with her."

Laura held me and forgiveness trickled down, melting all the hardness within me.

"I have to go back now."

"You're still taller than I am," I said irrationally.

"Well," she answered mildly, "that's one thing that won't change."

* * * * *

I landed in Milwaukee in the midst of the biggest snow storm in the past twenty-five years. I picked up my rental car at two in the morning but I was determined to get to Storm Lake seventy-two miles north. After being away for more than ten years, I couldn't wait. I slid sideways into a snowbank along with the other fools who had long abandoned their vehicles to the weather. I rummaged through my sparse supply of winter clothing and congratulated myself on bringing my cross-country ski gear with me. I pulled on my thigh-high wool stockings, my ski boots, and glided a half mile to the truck stop up the highway. I drank endless cups of coffee, played Pac Man with the truckers, and waited for my turn with the tow truck and the arrival of my brother-in-law.

The tow truck driver got there first. "I don't take credit cards."

We were at an impasse. I wanted to hang onto my cash. I swung myself up into the cab of his truck. His hair was blond as corn silk. His eyes were red. I asked, "How long have you been up?"

"Two, no three days, I think." He rubbed his eyes. "Where were you going?"

"Storm Lake," I replied. Our breath fogged the windshield.

"Oh yeah? I went to high school there."

174

"Me too! I graduated from St. Katherine's." Suddenly the cross-eyed bishop and the marble floors of St. Katherine's cathedral appeared in my mind's eye. I caught the scent of incense mingled with frosty air and cigarette smoke.

We examined each other, trying to establish if we had a common past, but he was behind me in school. Too young. "No shit!" he said finally, cracking his gum.

"No shit," I echoed.

"I graduated from Roosevelt." We pondered the Catholic kid and the public school kid rivalry of Storm Lake. "Got a check on you?"

"Sure do."

"I'll take that."

"Thanks." I knew I was back home in the Midwest.

With my car now safely parked in the truck stop lot, I settled back in for another cup of coffee and another game of Pac Man if I could locate somebody to play with me. I had just decided to ask the only other woman in the place when my brother-in-law, Karl, walked in the front door of the cafe. The minute I saw his face I knew he was going to enjoy every moment of this rescue. Small town boy saves big city girl.

"Well, such a deal, huh?" He grinned his broad, face-splitting grin at me and I remembered that I had always liked him. After all, he had been in love with DeeDee when she was twelve and he was thirteen and I had counted on that. Maybe I had brothers after all.

I invited him into my booth and he had coffee and hash browns and scrambled eggs. My California years were slipping away with the night and snow. When he was done he said, "Just drive in front of me and I'll get you there. Not used to the snow anymore, huh?" We went out into the chilled air and he stamped his feet and blew frost out of his red cheeks and laughed. He clapped his gloved hands together. "Just take it easy, okay?"

"Right," I affirmed and we drove ever so slowly down the slick highway ribbed with caked and blown snow. The wind whistled mercilessly across the prairie but I stayed on the road this time. Karl deposited me in my hotel room and went wearily away. I called DeeDee to report.

She laughed. "Sending my husband home?"

"Yes, thanks."

"We'll mention it in the morning." She guffawed.

"I'm sure you will."

I crawled into the cold white sheets and waited for morning. I was too tired to sleep.

Thanksgiving Day passed in a weary blur. We were all stupid with fatigue. Maggie had come in with her family and she celebrated the holiday at her in-laws' home. Tired travellers and their rescuers gathered around the turkey like bored pall bearers who have forgotten their purpose.

The next morning I waited impatiently for the snow plow to come around so I could drive across town to DeeDee's house. Another storm had moved in but now the sun was out and the new snow lay in a thirty-six-inch carpet of fluff. Eventually, as I inched my car down the slick streets, I marvelled at the snow-stained buildings of brick, wood, and stucco, the granite facades of the public buildings, the bare-branched trees above the frozen river, the stately and silent pines cloaked in snow. I sent positive thoughts to my snow tires and as I drove over the hump of snow in DeeDee and Karl's driveway, I wondered if I would be able to get out again.

"Don't worry about it," said Karl. "I can drive over anything, even in that." He gestured at my rental car.

"Hi," said DeeDee greeting me with her lopsided grin. She ducked her head shyly.

The two little ones, Pearl and J.J., looked me over as if they were trying to figure out if I could be put to any use. Even though Pearl was two years younger than J.J., they were

176

similar in size, height, and weight, with J.J. growing toward
middle childhood with his delicate slenderness and
lengthening of bone and Pearl at three still with her baby fat.
She was solid, with chubby knees, and stood with her feet
planted. J.J. was lithe and quick. Pearl wasn't so quick-silver.
She was determined. I passed scrutiny and by some mysterious
nonverbal decision-making process, they both grabbed me by
my pockets and dragged me off to Pearl's room. As I was
being carried away, I cried out to DeeDee, "Help! Help! I'm
being captured by dwarfs!"

I saw the love and mischief in DeeDee's eyes before the
door to Pearl's room slammed shut. They pushed me down to
the floor with them. While J.J.'s light quickness was in his
body, Pearl's was in her little voice and her new words. Pearl
showed me all of her treasures and J.J. danced around us,
happy to watch, cheer, and add local color. I saw every toy in
Pearl's closet. The teddy bears on her bed, the stuffed snake
under her bed, the dolls under her pillow. The children sat on
me. They laid on top of me. They rested their small heads on
my belly side by side and we all contemplated the ceiling for a
long quiet moment. DeeDee told me later that we were in
there for more than an hour. I wouldn't know. It was timeless.

Later that day, J.J. floated by in a cape and I could have
sworn that when he came down the four steps to the family
room that his feet never touched the floor. "Was he flying?" I
asked DeeDee.

DeeDee smiled. "He does have that effect on people."

In another corner, Pearl frowned in concentration over
papers, scissors, and pastes. "What's she doing?"

"Cutting and pasting," J.J. said. "She'll be at it for a long
time." He sighed with all of the superiority of old big brother
who's seen it all.

At that Pearl looked up and her ruddy cheeks and brown
eyes gleamed with a sudden inner radiance and then her head

went down again. The silky brown hair flowed forward on her neck as she cut out another flower from the Sunday magazine.

J.J. peered at my face and then announced, "Well, you do look like my Mom but you have lots more wrinkles."

"J.J.!" DeeDee shooed him out of the house. "Go do something!" He went off, nodding to himself. She watched him leave. "He's a good kid. Best on his ski team."

We settled down for a heart-to-heart at the kitchen table with coffee. "Still smoking?" I asked looking at the pack of Kents on the table top.

"Hell, yes. Not as much, though." She lit up. "I've got something to tell you."

"What?"

"I've changed my name."

"Huh?"

"Watch my lips. I've changed my name."

"Bitch!" I said cheerfully. "Okay, I'll bite. You've changed your name."

"Minerva," she announced, "And if you call me Minnie, I will never speak to you again." She blew out the smoke and watched me carefully.

"Minerva, it's ah. . . ."

"Unusual, I know."

"But that's the Roman name for Artemis or Diana, the Goddess of the Hunt."

"You know!" She cried it out in relief.

"Well sure. You might say I study goddesses all the time."

"I'm in therapy, you know."

"That's so great, Dee, I mean, Minerva."

"It's wonderful and terrible, just as you told me it would be. But anyway, do you know what DeeDee means?"

"No, I don't."

"It's Celtic and it's short for Deirdre and that means Lady of Sorrows." She looked at me triumphantly.

178

"Oh boy," I said, and then we were there again. To the heart and hurt of it.

Her chin came up. "There was this nun in high school, Sister Mary Theresa. She used to call me Minerva. She said I was wise. I always appreciated that and so I picked the name she gave me. Don't call me Minnie, though!"

"I promise."

Maggie blew in with a blast of cold air and the three of us went off to cross-country ski and to be alone together.

The sky was pewter gray. We hung over our poles while Maggie and new Minerva smoked their inevitable cigarettes. Maggie muttered, "Why the hell do you do this skiing, Annie? It's so much work." She threw the cigarette down and I watched it sputtering in the snow. "Some Thanksgiving we had yesterday."

I raised my eyebrow at Maggie. We were both avoiding telling Minerva about Kevin. I said, "We have something to talk to you about DeeDee. Minerva, I mean."

"About Kevin," Maggie said.

"No!" She dropped her poles and covered her ears. "My therapist says you should all get out of my face, and that's especially true for Kevin."

"We are going to see him while we are here," Maggie said, punching holes in the soft snow with one blue pole.

"I don't want to hear about Kevin, talk about Kevin, know about Kevin, or see Kevin right now. He's angry about that but it's just too bad. I told him to stay away from me."

I peered down the railroad tracks into the woods beyond. The trail had been laid out along the tracks by a snowmobile. The tracks curved into the bare branches of the wood. This was not the skiing of the high mountain meadows but prairie, lake and woodlands. It was all wonderfully flat. I wanted to glide away into the vanishing point but instead I asked, "Your therapist really said that?"

"What?" She pushed her chin out defiantly.

"Get out of your face?"

"Yes, so what?" She was trembling.

"I think I like her."

She pushed me and I fell into a snowbank. I caught her by the knees as I fell and brought her down with me. We wrestled and screamed. "Snow down your back if you don't stop!" I shouted, both mittened fists full of snow.

"Will you cut it out!" Maggie demanded.

Minerva and I exchanged glances, nodded and went after Maggie. "This isn't fair," she groaned as we put snow down her back and rolled her in the snow drifts.

Later, Maggie and I took Karl aside. "We think you need to know this, Karl."

"In case Kevin gets arrested," Maggie supplied.

"Arrested for what?" Karl's smile was gone now.

"He exposes himself to children in the park. I have no idea what he does in the winter."

"Kevin?"

Maggie nodded grimly. I met his eyes and he saw that we were serious. "We think you need to know so if it does hit the papers or something, you'll be able to be here for DeeDee . . . Minerva."

"Kevin?" he said again, stupidly.

"I know. It's hard to believe there's more on top of plain old child molesting, isn't it?" I shrugged cynically.

"But Minerva doesn't want to have anything to do with Kevin now." He looked for a way out, first in my face and then in Maggie's.

"We know," Maggie said.

He stood up. "I'll handle it. I'll take care of her."

"Thanks Karl. You've been a good brother all these years." I had never said this to him before.

"Sure," he mumbled. "Got to shovel out the driveway again before the snow gets too deep."

"Snow?" Maggie ran to the window. It was snowing again. "I've got to go or I'll never get back in time for dinner."

But it was too late. Maggie's car was stuck and not even Karl could drive it out. The tow truck wouldn't be by for another hour or so and we adjourned to the chairs in front of the fireplace. Maggie opened her mouth and Minerva gave her a warning glare but Maggie said, "It's not about Kevin. It's about Stella. She moved to Los Angeles and got an apartment near Brian. Can you believe that?"

"Sure," I said.

"I get it," Minerva agreed, peering into the fire.

"Well I don't!" Maggie turned her head from side to side waiting for the explanation. "After the letters and especially her own letter."

"You tell her, Annie."

"Love always," I said.

"Love always? What do you mean?" Maggie's eyes were now the color of the winter gray sky.

"That's the way she signed her letter. She is no more free of him than Carrie is. Something inside Stella is smashed. Maybe it's because there were two of them assaulting her. Maybe it's because it started when she was so little. Both Minerva and I were older when it started. Maybe that's why we've survived and she hasn't. Stella's gone. We've lost her, Maggie."

"No. I don't believe it. She can get therapy." Maggie moved toward Minerva for comfort.

"My therapist says Stella is what they call a borderline personality. It's not treatable by therapy. Nobody knows how to treat it." Minerva delivered this clinically, trying not to hurt herself with it.

Maggie shrank back from her but I went on, "You know how it is, Maggie. Just when you think you have a relationships with Stella, you realize you have to start over and over again every time."

181

"Yes," Minerva added. "You and I and Annie, we have history with each other. We build on what went before. We go on. With Stella there is no way to go on."

Maggie bowed her head in numb acceptance. She got up from the big wing-back chair and took a letter from her purse. "I got this from Kathleen for all of us."

Dear Maggie, Annie, and DeeDee,

I missed being with you in Los Angeles and I miss being with you in Storm Lake. I can't be with you and I'm not sure I want to be.

I am writing to clarify my relationships to Mother and to all of you.

I don't have any feelings of anger toward her for my childhood since I did not feel any need for her then. I'm feeling some anger toward her now about how she is dealing with your pain and I wish there was some way I could help all of you.

I love you but it is hard to understand your point of view. I am trying to see all sides but my experiences are so different that it is almost impossible. I am working on it and I hope you know you have my support to do what you must to make it good for yourselves.

I am sorry for Mother because she has lost the ability to face things and she is frightened and confused.

Love to you all,
Kathleen

"And so she keeps herself above the fray once again," I said. The vision came upon me: Kathleen as the Virgin of Guadalupe who rises up on her mountain top. Far above us all. Sending us her kindly consideration and her tender distress at our pain but she must leave us to our struggles.

182

"Kathleen is Lily at her best." Neither sister spoke. "Don't you think?" I urged.

Maggie stirred restlessly.

"You were supposed to be Mother's ideal woman at first, Maggie, remember? But then you rebelled and got a job and went to college and all that. You were supposed to be the perfect mother."

"Yeah," Minerva agreed absently, "I think that's true. And I was supposed to be her nun. The daughter given to the Church."

"But then who is Kathleen?" Maggie asked.

"Kathleen is the Lady," I answered and I remembered going to Polish Catholic Church with my Polish grandmother. I always loved going there because of the radiant statue of the Virgin in her blue robe with the golden hem. I reached out to her, that goddess with the golden hem, but like my mother, her hem was stone to me. I have no mother. But when the goddess/the Lady, is my sister Kathleen, I keep hope alive. I hope that the hem is silken, that it flows, that it ripples in the wind now blowing, that maybe under the blue robe is flesh, personhood. My sister, Kathleen.

"Yes, and who are you, Annie?" Minerva whispered.

I saw their expectant faces lit by the glow of the fire. "Oh, me? I'm Lily's dream of freedom." The fire burst and sparks flew onto the hearth and we jumped. There was a pounding at the front door. The tow truck had arrived and the moment was gone.

* * * * *

I woke at sunrise the next day. The window of my hotel room overlooked the river and one of the city's bridges. Only the birds were flying up from the still, bleak landscape. A snowplow rested on the bridge and there was no traffic, it was too early. But I was ready. I checked the time: seven o'clock.

183

Five minutes later, I checked it again but it wasn't moving any faster than it had before. I showered, shaved my legs, put on makeup, dressed. It was now seven-thirty-seven. I tried to slow down. I paced the suite. Back and forth, back and forth, watching the winter landscape and the clock.

As I restlessly prowled the rooms, I became aware that there was someone or something with me. It flickered in and out of my awareness at the same rate of my impatience with the clock, the bridge, the sleeping snowplow, the frozen river. It slipped into my conscious awareness coyly.

It was a snow shovel. A red snow shovel. The ribbed metal curves were painted candy-apple red and there was a long wooden handle of light wood.

Suddenly, in my innermost self, my hands raised the shovel high above my head and when it came down it bashed my father's dark-haired head into some sidewalk not quite free of snow. Ice cold as death. Smashing his head, and brains and blood pouring out. It was on the sidewalk or perhaps on a basement floor in one of those terrible basement bedrooms found only in the homes of the frozen winters of the northern Midwest.

I observed dispassionately that this was a peculiarly inefficient murder weapon. It didn't have the club-like possibilities of a coal shovel with its squared-off shape or the lethal edge of a garden spade with its pointed head. A snow shovel is designed to be lightweight and looks like the lost half of a large tin can cut sideways.

My red shovel was both cheerful and nasty. It danced merrily in my head as I telephoned Maggie. I could wait no longer.

"I've been waiting for you to call," she said.

"I'll come by and pick you up," I told her.

And as I drove the city of my youth, I realized that *he* had taken the town from me. The one and only time I had brought a friend to my house he had humiliated me by grabbing my breast and leering drunkenly at my new friend.

"This is my town too!" I said aloud, and the shovel did a little jig.

I didn't tell Maggie about the shovel but it was the three of us who went to our father's house where he lived with his second wife. The woman he finally married after living with her secretly for years. We did not call ahead.

"Now you let me start out," Maggie said. "Okay? We want to get what we want and you shouldn't just crash in there. Okay?"

"Okay, okay." I would have agreed to anything she asked of me. I was so grateful to have her there. The shovel bounced up and down gleefully. "Down!" I muttered.

"What?" Maggie asked. We were both tuned as tightly as piano wire and we could be twanged at the slightest touch.

"Nothing, I'm just glad you're here."

Clarisse, the new wife, answered the door. She was fat and old. *But she's only four years older than I.* She recognized Maggie at once. Everybody recognizes Maggie.

I introduced myself; we had never met. I was in my twenties by the time they had come into the open and married.

"Is Dad here?" Maggie asked.

"Yes, in here." She took us into the living room. Maggie walked in front of me and I watched my father's face light up as he recognized her. It was his old pleasure in her very existence, and it flowed through him from his father, who had had the same response to Maggie.

Then he spotted me behind her. His face changed. Fear swept over his features and I knew, for a moment, that he thought I was Lily. I understood, finally, that neither of my parents had ever seen me. To both I was some strange version of Lily.

But this time, I was myself to myself. I stood up very straight and looked calmly into his face without speaking.

"We would like to talk to you," Maggie announced.

"Well, sit down." He gestured feebly at the couch.

"No, we need to speak to you privately," Maggie insisted.

"Privately?" he asked with a raised eyebrow. He led us downstairs to the basement.

It was one of those basements in my darkest dreams. Dank, small, dark, with a window the size of a postage stamp. Even it would have a curtain, I was sure. I checked and there it was, shutting out the pale winter light glinting off snow in the back yard. A white curtain, trimmed with orange rickrack on the ruffles. The linoleum floor was covered by a rag rug. A furnace hulked brown and rusty off in the shadows. There was a couch on one axis of the long narrow space and a bunk bed on the short end. The walls were cinder block.

He walked slowly to the bunk bed and sat down on the lower level. I looked at him. I had not seen him for more than a decade.

His beauty was gone. He had become a dybbuk, a zombie. His hair and skin were the color of ashes. His scent was that of a cigarette butt lying in an ashtray overnight. His flesh was puffy at the wrists and cheeks and he moved slowly, as though his bones were unsure of their position inside his swollen skin. His breathing was labored. As though he dwelled in smoke and ashes.

I took my place on the long couch next to Maggie. I was content to let Maggie lead. She was the essence of sweet reason and motherly concern. The shovel and I waited confidently. Our turn was coming.

Maggie started. "We came here today to ask you about some things that happened in our family. We think it started generations ago and that it has been going on for a very long time."

I recognized the expression on his face. It was the weary patience of a martyr who must endure the prattling of fools. I was reminded of Lily.

"We wondered if you had any knowledge of it." Maggie paused, but he sat silently, leaving her with her words. "What I'm talking about is abuse. Sexual abuse."

"No!" He answered in quick surprise. I could see that his suspicion was building, but he had not caught on to us yet.

"Well, we think that Sue Ann had that trouble. Remember Frankie?" Maggie referred to our cousin and her father. "We think he molested her and that's why her life is such a mess."

Sue Ann was now a notorious drug addict. She roamed Storm Lake ransacking the medicine chests of anyone naive enough to let her into the house. She took Valium, Librium, Codeine, sleeping pills, Darvon.

He nodded comfortably. "Yes, that's true. I think you are right about that." His face was serious, concerned; and then it changed into a lascivious smirk. "Of course she was always ready to let everybody into her pants." He smiled, dismissing her.

The destruction of Sue Ann's life came before me in montage. Sue Ann diving from rocks seventy feet high. She had been a teenage athlete with a glorious young body. I remembered her water-skiing and pregnant with her first child, laughing. And then her deteriorating marriage to a battering husband, and the drugs. She had lost all of her children to him. I leaped up from the couch but Maggie's hand closed tightly around my wrist to pull me back.

"The abuse she suffered is the reason she is the way she is and we think it's in our family too." Maggie tightened her grip on my wrist.

"You do?" His tone was aggrieved.

I could wait no longer. I popped out of the couch on the springs in my legs and broke free from Maggie's grip. "Yes,

187

that's right. It happened to me. You molested me!" He stared at me dazed. "Don't you remember playing with my breasts in front of the television set after supper? You made me lie on the couch with you."

"Huh? I don't remember that." His mouth was set and his jaws were so tense that the flabby jowls had almost disappeared.

I was standing before him now. The shovel had vanished. I think it was inside me. I knew the meaning of hopping mad. "Well, you did it!" I shouted.

"I don't remember." He repeated stubbornly.

And then Maggie was on her feet beside me shouting too. "You were probably too drunk to remember!"

Pleasure rolled through me. I hadn't paid that much attention to the alcoholic chaos he had brought into the family because I had been so preoccupied by the incest and now here was Maggie's complaint. I cheered her on. "More, more!" I said.

She said it again, "You were too drunk to remember."

"I don't know what you're talking about," he said primly.

Maggie's Irish was up. Sparks were shooting from those blue eyes and that beautiful red hair. "What about all those times you made us sit in a car in the dead of winter outside some bar somewhere, for hours and hours on end?"

"What bars?" he shot back.

"The ones in Rice Lake, Eagle Flats, Greystone, Little Rye and Great Falls," I retorted, astounding myself with this list of villages. Taken aback by my specificity, we all paused. But I resumed the battle quickly. "You almost ruined my life. You molested me."

"I'm sorry," he said quietly.

I hadn't expected that and I drifted aimlessly on this sudden capitulation. I looked to Maggie for help but she was still seething with her own suddenly discovered anger. I felt collapsed.

But as I dithered, he said "My conscience is clear." He said it again. "My conscience is clear."

For a moment I was confused and then I got it. He had confessed it to a priest.

I got my spine back. I positioned myself directly in front of him. I let my arms fall loosely to my sides. Something slithered, uneasily rising from my pelvis up my spine through my belly to my chest, to my shoulders, down my arms and out through the palms of my hands. It slithered and crawled out of my body and fell in a heap at my feet. Behind it was a white light and the clear blue sky pushing it all out. And while this was happening, I chanted to him: "I came here today to give you a list. The consequences of your actions. I want you to have this list in your memory until the day you die. For all of this is your responsibility."

The heap at my feet crept over the braided rug and bound itself around my father's feet. "When you molested me, Bri was watching. You trained him. And what is he? A child molester, a wife beater and a torturer and despoiler of sisters. He raped Stella and molested DeeDee. Kevin, too. He raped Stella and Audrey, his own daughter. And now he exposes himself to children in the park."

He repeated, "My conscience is clear."

Maggie yelled, "It's true! It's all true!"

He remained seated. Tiredly, he said, "I'm not well. I haven't worked in a long time. I'm sick." He put his hand on his heart.

I leaped on this self-pitying whine. "You've always been on your death bed! I've been through your pneumonia, your asthma, your ulcers, your alcoholism, your hemorrhoids. And who cares?"

Clarisse came down the stairs drawn by the raised voices. She went to his side, putting her hand on his shoulder. "What's going on here? This man has a bad heart."

"Ain't that the truth?" I replied. "By the way, Clarisse, don't you two have a fourteen-year-old daughter? How is she?"

Clarisse shook her head in bewilderment. "She's fine."

"Has he molested her yet? She's just the right age."

"He would never do anything like that." Her face was white and strained.

"Oh yeah? Well, he did it to me. So you better watch out. Ask her. Ask your daughter." I could feel Maggie on fire behind me. My father was folding in on himself like a wet paper sack. "Maggie, are you finished?"

"Yes." She stamped her feet.

"Me too. I have nothing else to do here."

"Let's go then."

We moved toward the staircase and as we ascended, Clarisse emerged from her dazed silence. "You have a filthy mind! A filthy mind!" she screamed.

I laughed because I knew it wasn't me. It wasn't me. I wasn't the filthy one. It was him. I had left it all with him. The greasy ashes, the grimy smoke, the grinding banality of the evil he had poured into me so long ago with his probing fingers. I put my hand on the railing of the narrow staircase and it fell off the wall. This heightened my exultation. It was so fitting, so perfect. There was nothing to hang onto in my father's house! And the moment I set foot outside the door of that house, a scream rose and split the air with the force of a sonic boom. A scream so pure and full that Maggie covered her ears and I laughed again for the cleanliness of it. "Let him explain that to the neighbors," I said as I stood on the doorstep. I surveyed the blue sky and the virgin snow enfolding the suburban neighborhood in its cool and silent embrace.

"I'll drive." Maggie got into the driver's seat. She was panting, looking like a cat with a little pink tongue and hair standing on end.

"You were great, Maggie!"

190

"I didn't know I was going to yell at him. I didn't even know I was angry." She was filled with wonderment.

"You were wonderful!" I savored the moment. "Wasn't it perfect when the railing fell off?" We exploded into laughter.

"I liked it when you looked down at it in your hand and let it drop."

"And the way it slid all the way down the steps." This set us off again. When we stopped for breath I added, "Oh Maggie, I'm so glad I didn't have to kill him to be satisfied. Isn't that great? I feel immensely satisfied."

She gasped for air. "Oh, I didn't know."

"I didn't either until now." The shovel was back dancing a little jig. It didn't seem disappointed at all. I smiled at it and it went happily off to wherever it keeps itself.

She drove carefully as we passed through intersections lined with shoulder-high snowbanks. "I've made a decision, Annie."

"Oh? What's that?"

"I've thought it over and I think that I have to have a relationship with Mother."

"Yes."

She put on the turn signal. "I asked myself if she died tomorrow how would I feel?"

"And?"

"And I decided that I would have to have some sort of relationship. I also decided that I will not permit her to talk to me about you or anybody else. That's one of her tricks to divide us from each other." She made the turn. Her voice shook. "What do you think?"

"I think you're cracked," I said gently.

She took her eyes off the road for a moment to look at me. I suppose you would think that."

"But," I said, "your choice may prove to be more difficult than mine." Her shoulders sank down in relief. "I love you Maggie. You have to have your own relationship with Lily and with me. I don't have to agree with it but I'll respect it. Okay?"

"Okay."

And so it was a contract between us. She parked the car in front of Minerva's house. I kissed her on the nose. "Listen, we are the dynamic duo now, aren't we?"

She grinned. "Look at all the stuff we've done. We took care of DeeDee. I mean, Minerva, together in Los Angeles and—"

"The old man now. You were great and so was I!" I beat my chest happily.

"Are you done bragging?"

"Probably not. Why?"

"We still have Kevin to see."

"Oh yeah. Shit."

11

We met him at the cocktail lounge of the Holiday Inn that evening. His beer belly advancing before him as he walked, he led us to a table he had chosen far back in one corner near the window. Snow was falling again and we watched it swirl down from the night sky into the lamplight of the streets beyond.

His Robert Redford smile and good looks were still visible under the drinking and the overeating. I ordered club soda with a lime twist. Maggie had scotch and water and Kevin sucked on a bottle of beer. "I got a letter from Bri," he said, laying it on the table.

I picked it up. Fourteen hand-written pages. I skimmed through it. "Lawyer talk." I pushed it over to Maggie. My sympathy was with Kevin. Bri knew just how to manipulate him. Kevin had settled for a life without education or achievement. He wanted a steady job, a television set, beer, a faithful wife. It didn't matter to him if his kids went to college except maybe his son, who was, of course, more important than his daughters. He both distrusted and admired book learning and he was both flattered and angered by attention from people more educated than himself. Bri had pulled out his best vocabulary. The letter was designed to confuse and intimidate Kevin, the little brother. "Irony upon irony," I said.

"What?" Kevin was avid for my reaction.

"Lawyer talk," I repeated. "All crap, and the weird thing is Bri thinks the words are his but he's just Lily's mouthpiece. He's not free at all."

"You want me to choose between Mother and you," Kevin complained with a soft whine.

Maggie looked up quickly from her examination of Bri's letter. I shrugged. "I know that's what you think, Kevin. That's what you're supposed to think but do you know what?"

"What?'" he said reluctantly.

"I'm not your mother. I'm your sister. It's a false choice. I have resigned from the job of being Lily's foil. If you have problems with the parenting you received, take it up with your parents. Not me. I'm your sister."

"But Bri says you sisters can't forgive and forget." He reached across the table and took the letter from Maggie's hands. "Here, he says you should let the past be the past."

"We won't forget, ever, Kevin," Maggie challenged him and finally he looked away. His shoulders sank in disappointment.

"Tell me, Kevin, about you and Stella when you were little." My voice was gentle and receptive.

He took a long pull on the beer bottle. "Mother used to put us in bed together when Stella was sick. Stella used to try to stay home alone from school and then I'd pretend to be sick too." He smirked a little waiting for us to judge him.

194

When neither of us spoke, he continued. "I remember once I got in trouble with our next-door neighbor, Mrs. Riley. Remember that family?"

"Sure," said Maggie encouragingly.

"Mrs. Riley was upset because I'd been fooling around with Debby. I think Debby was five then and I was twelve, maybe thirteen."

"What happened?" I leaned forward so that I could see his face better in the gloomy light of the cocktail lounge.

"Oh, she complained to Mother." He tapped his cigarette on the edge of the amber glass ashtray.

"And what did she do?" Maggie was leaning forward too.

"Mother? Oh, she just laughed and said, 'boys will be boys.' "

"So what was the message, Kevin?"

"What do you mean?" He turned to me in alarm.

Maggie took up my question and repeated it measure for measure. "What was the message?"

He floundered looking from one face to the other and we told him in unison: "She told you it was okay to do that."

He raised his hand to the waitress, signalling for another round of drinks. He stubbed out his smoke and lit another. "You're probably right."

I didn't believe him. He was too smooth, too quick to agree. "What's wrong with Melody?" I said harshly.

"Nothing. Nothing at all. Why do you ask?" He was taken aback by this sudden change of topic.

Melody was his second daughter. She was unlike the delicate Audrey who was her mother's double. "Did you molest her too?" I was done with politeness.

"No, no! I didn't."

I decided it might be true. But when I had stopped by Kevin's house earlier I had become aware of the girl standing ponderously behind the dark wooden bar with its vinyl leather padding. I felt her before I even saw her. She was blonde like the rest of the family but she had inherited Kevin's thick body without his height. She drew me to her like a fire in darkness. I felt rage simmering in her. She evoked Stella for me. Stella at fourteen all those years ago. She wasn't like Audrey who had retreated behind a cheerful defense or Carrie who kept on smiling so that her face was dead to the touch.

"What's wrong with her?" I demanded.

He surrendered the information. "She was on the psych ward for six weeks about two months ago."

"What for?" Maggie's voice was filled with parental alarm.

He responded with the three unforgivable words. "I don't know."

"You don't know!" Maggie echoed in disbelief. "There had to be a diagnosis. What did the doctors tell you?"

He shifted heavily in the padded chair. "They said she was suicidal."

"Of course," I said more to myself than anyone else.

"What do you mean, of course?"

I could see he was actually surprised. I ached for Melody. I wondered if there was some way to pound awareness through his skull. "Look! I'm an adult female and I have a hard time being around for minutes. Your daughter has to be with you day after day. Year after year. She can't leave."

"Is she okay now?" Maggie wanted reassurance.

"Oh sure," he said easily, wanting to get out of it.

"How's Josie?" I was taking inventory.

"Who are you to ask me these questions?"

"I'm here because Maggie thought there might be some hope for you. I trust Maggie but I have my doubts. So if you want to relate to me, tell me the truth."

He gulped. "I never cheated on her, you know." He looked at me sideways to see what I would do.

"What are you talking about? You cheat on her all the time. On your way home from work when you flash. With your daughter. What are you talking about?"

196

He tried to please me. "I guess you're right."

"That's it, Kevin." I stood up. "I tell you what. Give me a birthday present."

"Huh?"

"If you want to have a relationship with me, I want a birthday present and this is what it is. Six months from now on May twenty-ninth. I want you to call me and tell me you have not been in the park flashing. I assume your child molesting has stopped but who knows? Your wife is a drunk, your oldest daughter is nuts and your middle daughter is suicidal. Your son is a perpetrator in training."

I put my sweater on. I was shaking with rage. I looked at Maggie sitting at the table.

"I'm staying a little longer," she said.

"You're lucky, Kevin. She believes in you still. Don't betray her trust." I picked up my purse. "By the way, don't bother lying to me. I can hear lies and so it won't do you any good."

I left the lounge and took the elevator up to my room where I stood in the shower for a very long time.

I was standing in the middle of my overheated bathroom dripping when the telephone rang. I grabbed a towel and answered. It was Maggie. "Hi."

"Hi." I wrapped the towel around me. It was white and scratchy from too much harsh laundering.

"We're leaving at five in the morning if we can get out of here. It's still snowing. I just wanted to say goodbye and tell you that I love you."

"I love you too, Maggie."

"He's pretty slimy, isn't he?"

"Yeah."

"I'm curious about something."

"What?"

"Remember how you and I and Minerva were talking about goddesses and stuff?"

"Yeah."

"Well, if I'm the Great Mother," she laughed a little, "then who is Stella and who is Mother?"

"Stella is the Great Whore," I said promptly. "She is Aphrodite or, in our times, Marilyn Monroe. Stella is the Marilyn Monroe of our family. Sex object and victim." I pulled the sheets back on the bed with the phone tucked between my ear and my shoulder. The towel fell to the floor.

"Do you think she'll die young like Monroe?"

I got into bed and pulled the covers up around me. I stuffed pillows behind my back. There weren't enough. "Yes, Maggie. I'm waiting for her to die."

"You are?" I heard the hurt in her voice.

"I'm sorry but what else is there for her?"

"It's so hard."

"Yes."

She shook that off with a cough. "And Mother?"

"I think Lily is Athena."

"Who's she?"

"She's the goddess who was born out of the head of Zeus the Father. She never had a mother. She is the goddess who chose father rights over mother rights in Greek mythology. She's always represented in armor." I thought of Lily imprisoned in her arthritic body.

"She never really did have a mother, did she?" Maggie's voice was filled with infinite sadness.

"No, I don't think she did."

"You've thought a lot about this, haven't you?"

"Yes."

"And what about you, Annie? Are you looking for a lover? Someone just for you?"

"I'm not ready to live with anybody if that's what you mean."

"I couldn't do it live by myself."

I settled myself happily into the pillows. "I've thought about this too. Remember when I bought the working drawing of the Natalie Barney Plate from Judy Chicago?"

"How could I forget? You actually have something from the Dinner Party Project. And Barney was that famous lesbian who lived in Paris in the nineteen-twenties."

"Very good. Anyway there's a quote from an interview with Barney. She says something about how her decision to live alone is not for any lack of love but in order to better give of herself. That's how I feel. Maybe it'll change but now "

"I love you, Annie."

"I love you, Maggie."

* * * * *

I slept well. I slept peacefully. I woke rested and when I pulled back the drapes the next morning at nine, I was astounded. There was snow and more snow. Three more feet, it turned out, on top of the layers and layers which had been falling since I had come to Storm Lake. I laughed out loud. The sun sparkled merrily in a clear sky. The radio announced a holiday. No school. No business. The town couldn't move.

I called Minerva. Karl answered. "Such a deal!" he said, explaining that he had just shovelled out the driveway and when he had gone back in to shave the snowplow had come by and left him with a four-foot snowbank. "Back to the old shovel one more time."

"Tell Minerva I'll be by in a couple of hours."

"How are you going to get here?"

"I'm skiing."

"Skiing?"

"Yup." I hung up. I hummed as I drew my thigh-high red wool stockings over my bright blue tights. I pulled waterproof red knickers over those. I put on a blue cotton turtleneck shirt with long sleeves and shrugged into my rainbow suspenders. I tied a wool scarf jauntily around my neck. I picked up my windbreaker, my fanny pack with an orange, money, and a small bottle of Perrier tucked inside. I slung the fanny pack and the jacket over my shoulder and picked up my long blue skinny skis, the poles dangling from the tips. I had a good time smiling at strangers in the elevator. I put the skis on in the parking lot where my car lay hidden under a mound of new snow.

I glided down the river road past my old high school. The snowplows were out but it would take them all day to free the town for normal traffic. I was the freest of all except, of course, for the snowmobiles. For once I forgave them their noise because they made such beautiful tracks for me in the streets. In some places the snow was so deep I sank to my waist even on the skis. I didn't care; I swam through the cool fluff. I thumbed my nose at the St. Katherine's high school as I went past, remembering how the principal had advised me to get a job as a waitress rather than go to college. "Screw you, you old bastard!" I shouted at the old priest's office as I left the brick building behind me. But no one was there.

I stopped and stuffed my windbreaker into my fanny pack and planned my route to Minerva's house five miles away. I sipped on Perrier. The sweat had emerged pleasantly all over my body and was pooling under my breasts. It was good to have the jacket off but I had to keep moving. The temperature was five degrees below zero. I switched head gear too. I put the blue wool stocking hat into the pack and zipped it up with difficulty. I slipped on the wool band to cover my ears.

I decided to follow the railroad tracks to the old house where so much had happened. My cousin lived there now. I didn't know her and she didn't know me, but as I glided up the carefully groomed driveway, I sensed that it would be okay. At the very least, it would give the Malloy clan something to gossip about. I grinned, wondering what they would make out of my strange visit. I double-poled up the incline of the groomed driveway and removed my skis, leaning them against the wall near the door.

Her name was Jean and she was around twenty-five years old. I explained who I was. She was a tired twenty-five-year-old and as I entered the shocking warmth of the house, I saw why. She had six children, two dogs, three adult cats, and two kittens who were lying in the clean laundry in the laundry basket. She glanced pointedly at my feet and I hastily removed my ski boots, explaining how the tips had holes in them so that the skis could be attached. Stocking footed, I was taken on a tour of the house.

It's just a house, I thought. There were new carpets and a new outside door and another bathroom, but it was still an old barn of a place with its narrow staircase and dry coal-heated air. I didn't stay long and I didn't say much. There was no need. Everything was finally over somehow. "I left something there," I told Minerva later. "I'm not sure what exactly. It wasn't like father, where all that stuff fell out. It was simple, final."

I went back to the railroad tracks and skied along the edges. I let peace settle into me like clouds moving into a clear sky or snow melting into itself. There were a few tricky intersections where the snowplow had actually managed to scrape down to the asphalt but as I went around the corner to Minerva's house, I saw that I would have to storm the driveway to get in. Karl had apparently taken the day off. As I side-stepped up the snowbank, Minerva burst out the front door with a camera. "Pose! Pose!" She shouted, pointing with the camera. I stood proudly on top of the mound.

Then she said, "I have a message for you from a woman named Kitty. She called from California."

"Kitty?" It couldn't be. Kitty was my attorney. "Kitty?" I took a chance and step-turned down the mound into the yard.

I hadn't taken any telemark skiing lessons yet. "Are you going to love this!" Minerva was bouncing with excitement.

"Tell me!" I demanded.

"Not till you get into the house," she teased, and darted through the front door.

I dropped my skis and quickly propped them against the wall of the house and ran in after her. I slipped out of my boots and sat down on the floor in the kitchen. "Well," I said, looking up, "what?"

"Kitty called to say she has a hot lead on finding your daughter."

"My daughter?" I whispered. I had one stocking off now.

"Your daughter." She smiled from her toes to her mouth. "You look stupid like that with one sock on and one sock off."

"Bitch," I told her fondly, staring at the red wool sock in my hand.

"Wait here."

"Okay." I wasn't going anywhere just yet. I pulled off the other sock and wiggled my toes. I was sitting on the floor with socks, ski boots, mittens, fanny pack and hats in piles around me. My back was against the wall.

She came back with a package. "Maggie and I weren't going to give this to you until Christmas but I think you should have it now." She was very pleased with herself.

I reached for the package which was wrapped every which way to Sunday. "How am I supposed to get this open?" I complained.

She brought me a pair of scissors and sat down on the floor with me, moving a kitchen chair to do so. Suddenly, it was deja vu. Minerva and I were small children together. Like Pearl and J.J. She watched me intently as I cut through the wrappings of paper and tape and string. Finally, there was a box and then the lid.

It was a teddy bear. A white teddy bear. A big white teddy the color of the moon. I hadn't known such teddies existed. She had round ears and the softest, deepest fur in the world. Warm brown eyes and nose. I took her reverently from her white tissue paper and held her to me. I put my face in her neck. I looked up at my sister. "How did you know?"

"Maggie told me," she said smugly, her knees drawn up. She hugged herself.

"Do you think I'm ready for this?" I asked humbly.

"Yes, I think you're ready for everything now."

Holding Moon Bear, I mused. "We are at the beginning now, aren't we?"

"Yes, Annie. We're at the beginning."

"Sister," I said.

"Sister," she echoed.

A few of the publications of
THE NAIAD PRESS, INC.
P.O. Box 10543 • Tallahassee, Florida 32302
Phone (904) 539-9322
Mail orders welcome. Please include 15% postage.

SEARCHING FOR SPRING by Patricia A. Murphy. 224 pp.
Novel about the recovery of love.   ISBN 0-941483-00-2 $8.95

DUSTY'S QUEEN OF HEARTS DINER by Lee Lynch. 240
pp. Romantic blue-collar novel.   ISBN 0-941483-01-0   8.95

PARENTS MATTER by Ann Muller. 240 pp. Parents'
relationships with lesbian daughters and gay sons.
                                        ISBN 0-930044-91-6   9.95

THE PEARLS by Shelley Smith. 176 pp. Passion and fun in
the Caribbean sun.   ISBN 0-930044-93-2   7.95

MAGDALENA by Sarah Aldridge. 352 pp. Epic Lesbian novel
set on three continents.   ISBN 0-930044-99-1   8.95

THE BLACK AND WHITE OF IT by Ann Allen Shockley.
144 pp. Short stories.   ISBN 0-930044-96-7 $7.95

SAY JESUS AND COME TO ME by Ann Allen Shockley. 288
pp. Contemporary romance.   ISBN 0-930044-98-3   8.95

LOVING HER by Ann Allen Shockley. 192 pp. Romantic love
story.   ISBN 0-930044-97-5   7.95

MURDER AT THE NIGHTWOOD BAR by Katherine V.
Forrest. 240 pp. A Kate Delafield mystery. Second in a series.
                                        ISBN 0-930044-92-4   8.95

ZOE'S BOOK by Gail Pass. 224 pp. Passionate, obsessive love
story.   ISBN 0-930044-95-9   7.95

WINGED DANCER by Camarin Grae. 228 pp. Erotic Lesbian
adventure story.   ISBN 0-930044-88-6   8.95

PAZ by Camarin Grae. 336 pp. Romantic Lesbian adventurer
with the power to change the world.   ISBN 0-930044-89-4   8.95

SOUL SNATCHER by Camarin Grae. 224 pp. A puzzle, an
adventure, a mystery—Lesbian romance.
                                        ISBN 0-930044-90-8   8.95

THE LOVE OF GOOD WOMEN by Isabel Miller. 224 pp.
Long-awaited new novel by the author of the beloved *Patience
and Sarah.*   ISBN 0-930044-81-9   8.95

THE HOUSE AT PELHAM FALLS by Brenda Weathers. 240
pp. Suspenseful Lesbian ghost story.   ISBN 0-930044-79-7   7.95

HOME IN YOUR HANDS by Lee Lynch. 240 pp. More stories
from the author of *Old Dyke Tales.*   ISBN 0-930044-80-0   7.95

EACH HAND A MAP by Anita Skeen. 112 pp. Real-life poems
that touch us all.   ISBN 0-930044-82-7   6.95

SURPLUS by Sylvia Stevenson. 342 pp. A classic early
Lesbian novel.   ISBN 0-930044-78-9   7.95

PEMBROKE PARK by Michelle Martin. 256 pp. Derring-do
and daring romance in Regency England. ISBN 0-930044-77-0   7.95

THE LONG TRAIL by Penny Hayes. 248 pp. Vivid adventures
of two women in love in the old west.   ISBN 0-930044-76-2   8.95

HORIZON OF THE HEART by Shelley Smith. 192 pp. Hot
romance in summertime New England.   ISBN 0-930044-75-4   7.95

AN EMERGENCE OF GREEN by Katherine V. Forrest. 288
pp. Powerful novel of sexual discovery.   ISBN 0-930044-69-X   8.95

THE LESBIAN PERIODICALS INDEX edited by Claire
Potter. 432 pp. Author & subject index.   ISBN 0-930044-74-6   29.95

DESERT OF THE HEART by Jane Rule. 224 pp. A classic;
basis for the movie *Desert Hearts.*   ISBN 0-930044-73-8   7.95

SPRING FORWARD/FALL BACK by Sheila Ortiz Taylor.
288 pp. Literary novel of timeless love.   ISBN 0-930044-70-3   7.95

FOR KEEPS by Elisabeth Nonas. 144 pp. Contemporary novel
about losing and finding love.   ISBN 0-930044-71-1   7.95

TORCHLIGHT TO VALHALLA by Gale Wilhelm. 128 pp.
Classic novel by a great Lesbian writer.   ISBN 0-930044-68-1   7.95

LESBIAN NUNS: BREAKING SILENCE edited by Rosemary
Curb and Nancy Manahan. 432 pp. Unprecedented autobiog-
raphies of religious life.   ISBN 0-930044-62-2   9.95

THE SWASHBUCKLER by Lee Lynch. 288 pp. Colorful novel
set in Greenwich Village in the sixties.   ISBN 0-930044-66-5   7.95

MISFORTUNE'S FRIEND by Sarah Aldridge. 320 pp. Historical Lesbian novel set on two continents.   ISBN 0-930044-67-3   7.95

A STUDIO OF ONE'S OWN by Ann Stokes. Edited by
Dolores Klaich. 128 pp. Autobiography.   ISBN 0-930044-64-9   7.95

SEX VARIANT WOMEN IN LITERATURE by Jeannette
Howard Foster. 448 pp. Literary history. ISBN 0-930044-65-7   8.95

A HOT-EYED MODERATE by Jane Rule. 252 pp. Hard-hitting
essays on gay life; writing; art.   ISBN 0-930044-57-6   7.95

INLAND PASSAGE AND OTHER STORIES by Jane Rule.
288 pp. Wide-ranging new collection.   ISBN 0-930044-56-8   7.95

WE TOO ARE DRIFTING by Gale Wilhelm. 128 pp. Timeless
Lesbian novel, a masterpiece.   ISBN 0-930044-61-4   6.95

AMATEUR CITY by Katherine V. Forrest. 224 pp. A Kate
Delafield mystery. First in a series.   ISBN 0-930044-55-X   7.95

THE SOPHIE HOROWITZ STORY by Sarah Schulman. 176
pp. Engaging novel of madcap intrigue.   ISBN 0-930044-54-1   7.95

THE BURNTON WIDOWS by Vicki P. McConnell. 272 pp. A
Nyla Wade mystery, second in the series. ISBN 0-930044-52-5   7.95

OLD DYKE TALES by Lee Lynch. 224 pp. Extraordinary
stories of our diverse Lesbian lives.   ISBN 0-930044-51-7   7.95

DAUGHTERS OF A CORAL DAWN by Katherine V. Forrest. 240 pp. Novel set in a Lesbian new world. ISBN 0-930044-50-9   7.95

THE PRICE OF SALT by Claire Morgan. 288 pp. A milestone novel, a beloved classic.   ISBN 0-930044-49-5   8.95

AGAINST THE SEASON by Jane Rule. 224 pp. Luminous, complex novel of interrelationships.   ISBN 0-930044-48-7   7.95

LOVERS IN THE PRESENT AFTERNOON by Kathleen Fleming. 288 pp. A novel about recovery and growth.   ISBN 0-930044-46-0   8.50

TOOTHPICK HOUSE by Lee Lynch. 264 pp. Love between two Lesbians of different classes.   ISBN 0-930044-45-2   7.95

MADAME AURORA by Sarah Aldridge. 256 pp. Historical novel featuring a charismatic "seer."   ISBN 0-930044-44-4   7.95

CURIOUS WINE by Katherine V. Forrest. 176 pp. Passionate Lesbian love story, a best-seller.   ISBN 0-930044-43-6   7.95

BLACK LESBIAN IN WHITE AMERICA by Anita Cornwell. 141 pp. Stories, essays, autobiography.   ISBN 0-930044-41-X   7.50

CONTRACT WITH THE WORLD by Jane Rule. 340 pp. Powerful, panoramic novel of gay life.   ISBN 0-930044-28-2   7.95

YANTRAS OF WOMANLOVE by Tee A. Corinne. 64 pp. Photos by noted Lesbian photographer.   ISBN 0-930044-30-4   6.95

MRS. PORTER'S LETTER by Vicki P. McConnell. 224 pp. The first Nyla Wade mystery.   ISBN 0-930044-29-0   7.95

TO THE CLEVELAND STATION by Carol Anne Douglas. 192 pp. Interracial Lesbian love story.   ISBN 0-930044-27-4   6.95

THE NESTING PLACE by Sarah Aldridge. 224 pp. A three-woman triangle—love conquers all! ISBN 0-930044-26-6   7.95

THIS IS NOT FOR YOU by Jane Rule. 284 pp. A letter to a beloved is also an intricate novel.   ISBN 0-930044-25-8   7.95

FAULTLINE by Sheila Ortiz Taylor. 140 pp. Warm, funny, literate story of a startling family.   ISBN 0-930044-24-X   6.95

THE LESBIAN IN LITERATURE by Barbara Grier. 3d ed. Foreword by Maida Tilchen. 240 pp. Comprehensive bibliography. Literary ratings; rare photos.   ISBN 0-930044-23-1   7.95

ANNA'S COUNTRY by Elizabeth Lang. 208 pp. A woman finds her Lesbian identity.   ISBN 0-930044-19-3   6.95

PRISM by Valerie Taylor. 158 pp. A love affair between two women in their sixties.   ISBN 0-930044-18-5   6.95

BLACK LESBIANS: AN ANNOTATED BIBLIOGRAPHY compiled by J.R. Roberts. Foreword by Barbara Smith. 112 pp. Award winning bibliography.   ISBN 0-930044-21-5   5.95

THE MARQUISE AND THE NOVICE by Victoria Ramstetter. 108 pp. A Lesbian Gothic novel.   ISBN 0-930044-16-9   4.95

OUTLANDER by Jane Rule. 207 pp. Short stories and essays by one of our finest writers.   ISBN 0-930044-17-7   6.95

SAPPHISTRY: THE BOOK OF LESBIAN SEXUALITY by
Pat Califia. 2d edition, revised. 195 pp.   ISBN 0-930044-47-9   7.95
ALL TRUE LOVERS by Sarah Aldridge. 292 pp. Romantic
novel set in the 1930s and 1940s.   ISBN 0-930044-10-X   7.95
A WOMAN APPEARED TO ME by Renee Vivien. 65 pp. A
classic; translated by Jeannette H. Foster. ISBN 0-930044-06-1   5.00
CYTHEREA'S BREATH by Sarah Aldridge. 240 pp. Romantic
novel about women's entrance into medicine.   0-930044-02-9   6.95
TOTTIE by Sarah Aldridge. 181 pp. Lesbian romance in the
turmoil of the sixties.   ISBN 0-930044-01-0   6.95
THE LATECOMER by Sarah Aldridge. 107 pp. A delicate love
story.   ISBN 0-930044-00-2   5.00

ODD GIRL OUT by Ann Bannon   ISBN 0-930044-83-5   5.95
I AM A WOMAN by Ann Bannon.   ISBN 0-930044-84-3   5.95
WOMEN IN THE SHADOWS by Ann Bannon.
                                    ISBN 0-930044-85-1   5.95
JOURNEY TO A WOMAN by Ann Bannon.
                                    ISBN 0-930044-86-X   5.95
BEEBO BRINKER by Ann Bannon   ISBN 0-930044-87-8   5.95
    Legendary novels written in the fifties and sixties,
        set in the gay mecca of Greenwich Village.

VOLUTE BOOKS

JOURNEY TO FULFILLMENT   Early classics by Valerie   3.95
A WORLD WITHOUT MEN   Taylor: The Erika Frohmann   3.95
RETURN TO LESBOS   series.   3.95

These are just a few of the many Naiad Press titles—we are the oldest
and largest lesbian/feminist publishing company in the world. Please
request a complete catalog. We offer personal service; we encourage and
welcome direct mail orders from individuals who have limited access to
bookstores carrying our publications.